INVITATION

TO ALL COUPLES IN LOVE

We, the citizens of Eternity, take great pleasure in inviting you to hold your wedding at the Powell Chapel.

Remember the legend: Those who exchange their vows in the chapel will remain together for the rest of their lives.

So let us help plan your special day. We've been making dreams come true for more than a hundred years.

Weddings, Inc.

Eternity, Massachusetts

Weddings, Inc.

Join us every month
in Eternity, Massachusetts...where love lasts forever.

June 1994	WEDDING INVITATION by Marisa Carroll (Harlequin Superromance #598)
July 1994	EXPECTATIONS by Shannon Waverly (Harlequin Romance #3319)
August 1994	WEDDING SONG by Vicki Lewis Thompson (Harlequin Temptation #502)
September 1994	THE WEDDING GAMBLE by Muriel Jensen (Harlequin American Romance #549)
October 1994	THE VENGEFUL GROOM by Sara Wood (Harlequin Presents #1692)
November 1994	EDGE OF ETERNITY by Jasmine Cresswell (Harlequin Intrigue #298)
December 1994	VOWS by Margaret Moore (Harlequin Historical #248)

If you miss any of these WEDDINGS, INC. stories, get in touch with Harlequin Reader Service:

In the U.S.

3010 Walden Avenue
P.O. Box 1369
Buffalo, NY 14269-1369

In Canada

P.O. Box 609
Fort Erie, Ontario
L2A 5X3

EXPECTATIONS

Shannon Waverly

Harlequin Books

TORONTO • NEW YORK • LONDON
AMSTERDAM • PARIS • SYDNEY • HAMBURG
STOCKHOLM • ATHENS • TOKYO • MILAN
MADRID • WARSAW • BUDAPEST • AUCKLAND

Kathleen Shannon is acknowledged as the author of this work.

ISBN 0-373-03319-2

EXPECTATIONS

This edition published by arrangement with Harlequin Enterprises B. V.

Printed in U.S.A.

Weddings, Inc.
DIRECTORY

Your guide to the perfect Happily-Ever-After

BRIDAL CONSULTANT	Bronwyn Powell
INVITATIONS & STATIONERY	Jennifer Thompson
ANTIQUES & GIFTS	Patience Powell
HAIR SALON	Dodie Gibson
CATERER	Manuel Silva
BRIDAL GOWNS	Emma Webster
FLORIST	Julianna Van Bassen Marguerite Van Bassen
LIMOS	Daniel Murphy
FORMAL WEAR	Ted Webster
RECEPTION/ACCOMMODATION	Lincoln Mathews
TRAVEL AGENCY	Jacqui Bertrand
PHOTOGRAPHER	Sarah Powell
LINGERIE, ETC	Christine Bowman
JEWELRY	Marion Kent
BAKERY	Lucy Franco
GIFTS	Jean Stanford
FABRIC	Marg Chisolm
SHOES	David Guest
BAND	Kerry Muldoon

Dear Reader,

When my editor called to inquire if I'd be interested in contributing to a new cross-line series set in Massachusetts, I wondered, "Does she really have to ask?" Having lived in Massachusetts all my life, I absolutely love the area, and one of my greatest joys is sharing it through my writing.

Another draw was the core element of this series, the wonderfully romantic legend of the Eternity chapel. To be honest, I was skeptical at first. A chapel that guarantees happiness to all marriages performed within its walls? Who in the 1990s was going to buy that idea? But, as often happens, my skepticism became my ally in writing *Expectations*, because it forced me to examine the nature of myth and acknowledge its value—*especially* in the 1990s.

But perhaps the most irresistible lure of all was the challenge of writing Geoff and Marion Kent's story. Married ten years, they are the first chapel couple to separate. I'd never written a romance about a married couple before and had read very few. Romance novels usually end with the hero and heroine *about* to be married, *about* to ride off into the happily-ever-after. But what happens a decade down the road, when "ever after" isn't quite what the couple expected? I wondered, was a romance even possible between two such characters?

Believe me, it was a challenge I won't easily forget (nor will my family, who've dubbed the time I spent writing this book "The Eternal Summer," because I was eternally at the computer). Somewhere along the way, however, writing *Expectations* also turned into a labor of love, a joyful commitment to answering that, yes, romance is not only possible in marriage, it's better.

I hope you enjoy *Expectations* and will continue reading the Eternity series. After all, Geoff and Marion's story doesn't *quite* end with this book.

All the best,

Shannon Waverly

CHAPTER ONE

MARION KENT couldn't ever remember not wanting to see her sister, but when she glanced up from the antique brooch she was repairing at the rear of her shop and saw Robyn waltzing through the door, she actually muttered an audible "Oh, no!"

Fortunately Robyn didn't hear it. "Hey, sis!" she called, beaming more cheerily than seemed humanly possible.

Marion broke into a reluctant smile, the first of the day—maybe of the week—and she thought, of course she was glad to see her sister. It was precisely because she loved her so much that she'd momentarily been distressed.

Marion came around the counter and the next moment was caught in an exuberant hug. "Why didn't you call and tell me you were coming?"

"What? Do I need an invitation these days?"

Laughing, Marion stepped back. What a beautiful young woman her twenty-four-year-old sister had become. They both had their mother's honey-blond hair, but unlike Marion, who kept hers long and naturally straight, Robyn's was a stylish froth of short curls. They both had their father's bright sapphire eyes, too, but Marion, though only seven years older, felt as washed-out as Robyn was radiant.

"How are you, sis?" Robyn asked with a sliver of concern in her voice.

If only Robyn knew what a loaded question she was asking. *I'm angry,* Marion wanted to shout. *I'm angry and bitter and so hurt I could die.*

"Great," she replied, walking her sister farther into the shop. All around them, lighted glass cases gleamed with brilliant gemstones, silver and gold. On the outside, Center Jewelers exuded a quaint New England seacoast charm, as did all the shops in the small business district of Eternity, Massachusetts. In reality this was one of the finest full-service jewelry stores north of Boston. Marion employed four clerks part-time to keep it running.

Her parents had owned the store before her, and it was here that she'd developed her love for beautiful things. This love had led her to become not only the store's proprietor when her parents retired, but also a jewelry designer whose reputation was growing by leaps and bounds.

"Have you had lunch yet?" she asked her sister.

"Stopped on the highway. But I sure could use a cold drink. Must be the warmest June we've ever had. This air-conditioning really feels good." Robyn spread her arms and let her eyes drift closed. Like a bird gliding on a breeze, Marion thought, watching her turn dreamily side to side in the cool air.

But even as she was enjoying Robyn's evident happiness, her own mood sank. Her marriage, which had been quietly deteriorating for the past couple of years, had finally fallen apart. Well, not fallen. More like exploded. After ten years, Geoff had walked out, and she still hadn't told any of her family. Maybe Robyn's unexpected visit was a sign that it was time.

But how? Marion wondered, heading for the small refrigerator in the back room. The thought of saying the words was painful. It would lend the separation a reality she still had trouble grasping herself, and today for some reason she'd awakened in an unnaturally melancholy mood, her eyes brimming over just at the thought of Geoff—which she knew was perfectly ridiculous. After the way he'd betrayed her, she should be glad to see him go. She *was* glad, she told herself.

Marion returned with two frosty cans of soda and handed one to Robyn. "So, how are things in Newport?"

"Glorious." Robyn popped the top of her soda and cast Marion a grin.

"And how is private duty working out for you?" Marion dropped into the chair behind the desk and waved Robyn toward a matching seat in front.

"Believe it or not, I went back to the hospital. I missed the excitement. Been back three weeks, in fact. Has it been that long since we talked?"

Marion fixed her gaze on the top of her desk. With her marriage coming apart, she hadn't really wanted to talk to anybody. She used to regret the hundred miles that separated her and Robyn, but not recently. Distance had been an ally, helping her to keep her marital problems a secret. Her parents, who had moved from Eternity all the way to Florida, were even easier to keep in the dark.

"How's Nate?"

Robyn's smile warmed her whole face. "He's the reason I'm here." For several seconds, she stared at Marion, her eyes gleaming. Marion's nerves began to ring.

"What?" she asked cautiously.

"He... he's asked me to marry him."

"No!"

"Yes!"

Marion couldn't move. A part of her wanted to let loose a jubilant shriek, but another part, the part that was crushed and embittered, wouldn't let her. "And did you accept?"

"Did I *what?*"

Marion shrugged, feeling foolish for having asked.

"Only problem is, he's being restationed to Texas in just over four weeks."

"Oh, Rob. What are you going to do? Does he expect you to just pick up and follow him out there?"

Robyn looked a little puzzled. "Well... yes. Besides, I want to go."

Marion's breath quickened. She'd been so like her sister when she and Geoff were engaged. She would have followed him into the jaws of hell armed with only a water pistol if he'd asked.

"Does that mean the family will have to fly halfway across country for your wedding?"

Robyn's puzzlement deepened. Marion suddenly realized how rude and selfish the question sounded. She should be congratulating her sister, telling her how happy she was for her, instead of throwing a damper on her joy with this misplaced resentment. So what if her own marriage was simultaneously ending? That was an irony she could brood over later. Alone.

"No, nobody has to fly to Texas. You see, we want to be married before he's restationed—here in Eternity. That's the problem."

"Here? In four weeks?" Marion sat bolt upright. *Oh, Lord. Not now. Not here.* "What sort of wedding do you expect to pull together in four weeks?"

"As nice a one as possible. But I'm a realist. I know we'll have to compromise on lots of things."

"We?"

Robyn smiled her most winsome. "Well, since you know just about *everybody* on the wedding circuit here in town, I thought maybe..."

"I could pull the wedding together for you?" Marion felt her color drain.

"Not alone. I'd help every step of the way. I just thought with you being a member of Weddings, Inc., you could cut through a lot of red tape."

Weddings, Inc. was an association of local merchants, all involved in the bridal business. Marion's friend, Bronwyn Powell, had organized them, and they now boasted a member roster long and diverse enough to fill the needs of any and every wedding that took place in Eternity.

Marion sat back, her breath hissing like a slow tire leak. "Are you absolutely determined to have your wedding here?"

"Yes, of course. You know I've always wanted to be married in the Powells' chapel. Where else?"

Where else, indeed? Very few girls born and raised in Eternity escaped the fairy-tale lure of that little stone chapel on the Powells' estate, and studying Robyn's expression,

Marion sensed she was facing a believer more zealous than most.

The Powells, one of Eternity's most prominent families, had come to America in the mid 1800s and had built a private chapel on their farm reminiscent of the country churches they'd left behind in their beloved Wales. Within a short time a romantic legend grew up around the chapel, a legend that claimed that no marriage solemnized there ever ended unhappily. The legend spread, and for more than a century now, couples had been traveling to Eternity to be married. In recent years they'd come in ever-increasing numbers and from every corner of the globe.

Only trouble was, the legend was all a hoax, a gimmick perpetuated by the Chamber of Commerce whose only interest lay in the profits that poured into town from gullible young lovers seeking an ironclad guarantee that their rose-colored glasses need never come off. Marion should know. After all, she'd been married in the chapel, too, and look what had happened to her marriage.

"How about Newport?" Marion tried. "A military wedding can be stunning."

Robyn not only looked perplexed again, she also sounded hurt as she said, "How can you even suggest such a thing?"

"Well—" Marion groped for a gracious escape "—the chapel might be all booked up."

"I'll be happy with whatever time is available. I'm not taking any chances with my marriage." She paused, frowning. "Marion, don't you want me to be married in the chapel? Don't you want my marriage to last and be happy like yours?"

"Oh, honey, of course I do. I wish you all the best." The idea that Robyn thought she didn't wish her well pained her. She absolutely adored this sister of hers. From the moment their mother had come home from the hospital with her, Marion had adopted Robyn as *her* baby. "And... and I'll help you in any way I can."

As soon as the words were out, Marion winced. By agreeing to help, she'd just guaranteed that her sister would be married in Eternity.

Which meant she'd have to tell her family that she and Geoff had separated, and she'd have to tell them soon.

She dreaded that—having to say the words, having to suffer their pity and endless questions. But what distressed her even more was knowing she would be upsetting them. Geoff had been part of the family for twelve years, if you added in the two he and Marion had dated. They were all going to be hurt and saddened and plunged into worry when they heard about the breakup, which was a terrible thing to do to people who were supposed to be celebrating a wedding.

"Thanks, sis." Robyn beamed. "And I mean it, I'll help too."

"Will you be wanting Bronwyn to officiate?" Among her other accomplishments, Bronwyn was also a justice of the peace.

"Yes, of course."

"So, what do you plan to do in Texas? Are there any hospitals near the base where you can work?"

"Uh-huh. But I only plan to do that for about a year. Then it's rug-rat time." She flashed another wide smile. "As soon as possible I want to stay home and start making babies, lots of them." Immediately a stricken look came over her. "Oh, Marion, I'm sorry."

Marion waved a dismissive hand and tried to look mildly irritated that anyone should feel uncomfortable talking about babies in her presence.

"It really doesn't bother you?"

"Really, it doesn't. Geoff and I have fully accepted our condition and gone on with our lives." No, *my* condition, Marion amended silently.

"Well, it still might happen, who knows? And if it doesn't you can always adopt."

Not likely, Marion thought, considering the fact that she no longer had a live-in husband. "Hey, this isn't the sort of thing we should be discussing today."

"Right. I have a million errands to run." Robyn seemed relieved. "Before I go, though, I have another favor to ask." Her happiness was back and radiating in palpable waves. "Nate and I would like you and Geoff to be our matron of honor and best man."

Marion's stomach bottomed out. "I...I'm not sure that's p-possible, Rob."

"But you're my only sister. Ever since I was old enough to pin one of Mom's curtains on my head and play bride, I always pictured you as my attendant."

Marion chewed on her lip. "Of course, I'd be honored. But surely Nate has someone closer to him than Geoff. A childhood friend? Someone in the navy?"

"Sure, but he wants Geoff. He really admires him, and well, we both think of you as the most fantastic couple we know. With the two of you standing at the altar beside us, we're hoping some of your magic will rub off."

Marion rose from her chair and, clutching her arms, paced to the front door. Her eyes were turning hot again, her throat closing.

From behind her, Robyn continued, "Nate and I realize our wedding won't be perfect. At this late date we'll be lucky to get the rec room at the fire station for our reception, but we can live with that. What we can't live with is not having you and Geoff in our wedding party. You're our role models, sis. Don't you realize that?"

Don't say that, Robyn, Marion pleaded silently. *We're not what you think.* She fixed her blurred vision on the row of frame-house shops baking in the summer heat on the opposite side of First Street. Three doors up, at a diagonal, was Geoff's office, the shingle over the door reading Geoffrey Kent, Attorney At Law. Marion's eyes lifted automatically to the windows of his second-floor suite.

For one unguarded moment she let herself miss the early years of their marriage, when more often than not he'd appear at one of those windows if she happened to be standing here as she was now, and they'd press their hands against their respective panes of glass and feel their love connecting them, their longing sizzling across the busy divide.

"Hey, I'm not allowing any tears at this wedding," Robyn chided good-naturedly. Marion hadn't heard her get up. "So you can just turn off the waterworks right now."

Marion smiled. "Yes, ma'am."

Robyn glanced across the street, an impish smile entering her eyes. "Okay, now to break the news to Geoff. I'm dying to see his expression."

"Wait! Robyn!"

Robyn yanked her hand from the doorknob. "What?"

"Uh..." Marion's pulse pounded. "He's...not there."

"How come?"

"Well, he's...gone to Boston today."

"Oh." Robyn rumpled her curls. "What am I going to do now? Nate's at sea for two weeks. He asked if I'd talk to Geoff."

Marion told herself the situation had gone on long enough. She had to enlighten her sister. Now.

She opened her mouth—but one look into those trusting blue eyes and she knew she couldn't do it.

"I'll pass along your request tonight when he comes home. How's that?"

Robyn's disappointment cleared, replaced by her usual animation. "Great. Oh, I almost forgot—I have one more favor to ask. Do you have time to design our wedding rings?"

Inwardly Marion balked. Between her hours at the store, her current jewelry-making commitments and her involvement with the Open Space Committee, she barely had enough time to breathe. And quite frankly, she wasn't in the right frame of mind to design a wedding band, that quintessential symbol of marriage.

On the other hand, she'd made hundreds of rings for strangers. In fact, her handcrafted wedding bands were her specialty. How could she possibly refuse her own sister?

"Do you have anything in mind?"

"Vaguely."

"Why don't you have a seat, then, and look through my catalogs. Let me know when something strikes you. Of course, I never make two sets exactly alike."

"I know. Because no two marriages are ever alike, right?"

"Right." Marion became aware that while she'd been talking she'd been turning her own wedding band round and round. It was the first one she'd designed, and while she'd gone on to do better work, no ring had ever been made with more love or care.

She gazed at the intricate pattern, two intertwining and inseparable rose vines etched into a wide gold band. She'd been quite a believer herself at twenty-one. In symbols, in legends, in happily-ever-afters.

Fleetingly she wondered if Geoff was still wearing his, or if he'd already tossed it into a drawer to become forgotten among his socks. Worse, had he thrown it away?

"Hey, Marion, you all right?"

"What? Oh, yes, fine. Go on and look through my books." A customer had just entered. "I'll be with you as soon as I'm free."

Twenty minutes later the customer had made her purchase and Robyn had chosen a design. After giving Marion her own and Nate's ring sizes, she headed for the door.

"Well, I'm off to the gown shop. Can you come with me? We have to find a dress for you, too."

Marion glanced over her shoulder. Several people were browsing, nothing her salesclerk who'd just returned from lunch couldn't handle by herself, but suddenly Marion knew she had another job that needed doing, fast.

"Not right now, Rob. We're a bit backed up here. I'll catch up with you in about half an hour."

"Okey-doke." Robyn fairly danced out to the sidewalk. "See you then."

As soon as she was gone, Marion hurried to the back room and shut the door. She had to warn Geoff that Robyn was in town. If he ran into her and spilled the news of their breakup, Robyn would be devastated.

As she picked up the phone a wave of nausea washed through her. She dropped the receiver and bent over, clutching her stomach.

Not only had she not seen Geoff in the six days since he'd left, they hadn't even spoken. Now the thought of calling him filled her with an image so vivid she actually felt sick—the image of walking into his office and finding him locked in an embrace with another woman.

She took a few calming breaths, and when she felt a little steadier, she picked up the phone again. With a hand that visibly shook, she pressed the buttons marked Auto and 1, then listened to the number programmed into the phone tumble through its sequence.

"Geoffrey Kent, Attorney at Law. How may I help you?"

"Freddie? Hi, it's Marion." She waited for the receptionist's usual bouncy rejoinder, but today heard only silence.

Finally, "Y-yes?"

Marion drew a shallow breath. Did Freddie know about the split? Was Geoff *telling* people?

"Is Geoff there, by any chance?"

"Yes, he is. Do. . . do you want to speak with him?"

Marion clutched the top of her head. What did Freddie think she wanted? "Yes."

"Just a minute. I'll see if he's available." She put Marion on hold.

Marion squeezed her eyes shut. She knew Geoff screened his calls—but not her, never her.

Several long seconds passed. Her heart thumped harder with each one. Finally the line opened again. Another second passed, two, three, four, five. Instinctively she knew it was Geoff at the other end of that silence.

Was he as lost for words as she was? As lost for a way to cross the wasteland they'd created of their marriage?

Finally, "Hello, Marion." His voice was calm, cool and impossible to read—the ultimate lawyer voice.

"Hi." Hers wasn't. It was high and thin and spoke volumes about vulnerability.

The line hummed with silence again. She hadn't a clue what to say next. She thought about the usual questions a person asked to get a conversation started: How are you? What's new? What've you been up to? But considering their circumstances, those questions suddenly seemed to take on new and decidedly uncomfortable connotations.

"What do you want, Marion?" Geoff asked. She got the feeling he'd been running down the list of conversation starters himself and had settled on this as the least ludicrous.

What did she want? Marion frowned as she tried to concentrate. What did she *want?*

Unexpectedly she felt a hysterical laugh swelling inside her. She *used* to know what she wanted, used to be so certain. She'd simply wanted to be Geoff's wife to the end of her days, to share his life, provide a comfortable home for him and the half dozen children they'd planned to have, to travel with him down the decades, as blissful at the end as they were in the beginning.

Now all she wanted was to stop hurting, to stop feeling this rage. She wanted to turn the clock back twelve years, back to the summer day she first laid eyes on Geoff, when he was the new guy in town all the girls were talking about. She wished she could take back her smile, decline his invitation to the wharf dance—and reclaim her ravaged life.

"Marion?"

"I...I need to talk to you, Geoff. It's important. I wouldn't be calling you at the office if it wasn't. I hope you know that." She also hoped her voice conveyed the fact that she didn't want to argue. They could be angry and resentful later, but for now she needed a truce. "Can you talk?"

"Yes, but not for long. Two or three minutes tops. I have a client waiting downstairs."

"Oh...uh..." She'd never get everything said in three minutes. But not telling him wasn't wise, either. "I hate to break the news this abruptly, Geoff, but Robyn and Nate have decided to get married."

She waited through a long pause. Geoff had a deep affection for Robyn and Nate, and under happier circumstances he would've been laughing or hooting in surprised joy. "Have they set a date?" he asked evenly. It hurt to realize she'd become someone he tempered his reactions with.

Quickly she explained the time crunch imposed by Nate's impending transfer. *This* finally elicited an unguarded response.

"That damned Eternity chapel!" he said. "They're rushing into the most serious contract of their lives and turning everyone else's life upside down in the process. And why? Just so they can be married in that foolish chapel."

"I know, I know," she commiserated. Their marital problems had united them in at least one area: they'd both lost their fondness for the legend.

"I have to ask—what was Robyn's reaction to our split?"

Marion was a little amazed to hear him talking about their separation so conversationally. Putting a third party between them was probably what made it possible.

"She, um, doesn't know yet. I haven't told any of my family." Actually she hadn't told anyone, except Bronwyn. For one thing, the pain was too new, the anger too raw. But more importantly lots of people in Eternity depended on weddings for their livelihood, and she didn't want to be responsible for undermining their source of income.

In her darkest moments, she even feared an upsurge of community anger toward her and Geoff. They would be the first couple married in the chapel to break up, at least the first that anyone had heard about, and the news wasn't going to sit well with the citizens of Eternity—or with anyone else who believed in the legend, for that matter. Debunking a cherished myth was a lot like messing with a cosmic force.

Geoff thought quietly a few seconds. "Oh, now I understand this call. Robyn wants to invite me to the wedding, right?"

"No."

"No?" He sounded surprised and a little hurt.

"More than just invite." She gulped. "Robyn and Nate... they want... they want us to be—" she squinched her eyes before finishing "—their attendants."

"You're kidding." His voice dropped like a rock down a well. She imagined his heart was doing the same.

"Wish I was."

"You said no, of course."

"Not exactly."

"Not exactly." His breath quickened. "You mean you said *yes?*"

"Well..."

"Marion, how could you? How the hell are we supposed to be in their wedding party when we're not even together anymore?"

"I don't know!" she snapped, his impatience igniting hers. "Right now, I don't know anything. All I can say is I *will* tell them. I will. I can't get out of being Robyn's matron of honor, but I'll get you off the hook, I promise. In the meantime you might want to keep a low profile. That's why I'm calling—to warn you Robyn's in town. She'll be shopping in the First Street area for the next couple of hours."

"Oh."

"But if you do happen to run into her, will you please not tell her about our separation. I'd rather do it myself in my own good time."

He groaned. "I don't need this right now."

"You think I do?" Her voice leapt.

"Calm down, will you? I don't want to argue on the phone."

"Oh? Where *do* you want to argue?" Marion suddenly heard herself and sucked in a breath. "Sorry. I don't want to argue, either."

"It's okay. We're both pretty stressed out." He sounded tired, and Marion wondered what sort of week he'd had. "Listen," he continued, "I need to stop by the house to pick up some more clothes. How about we continue this discussion tonight?''

''Tonight?'' She drew up sharply. ''You'll be coming to the house tonight?''

''Yes. About seven-thirty, seven-forty-five. I have to attend a planning-board meeting first.'' When several seconds elapsed and she didn't respond, he added, ''Do you have a problem with that?''

''No, no. In fact, I have to be at the same meeting.''

''With the Open Space Committee?''

''Yes.''

''Regarding the Borden farm?''

''Yes.''

''I guess I'll see you there, then.''

''I guess you will.'' Marion replaced the receiver and clutched her arms. The back room was quiet and still, but one of Geoff's sentences kept echoing all around her. He was coming to pick up more clothes.

If she'd ever had any doubts about where he was heading with this separation, his intentions were now crystal clear.

THE PLANNING BOARD held its meetings every Thursday at seven o'clock in the conference room on the second floor of the Town Hall on Soldier's Green. In essence, anyone who wanted to do anything with real estate in the town of Eternity had to present their petition to this board. Likewise, anyone who disputed a proposed real-estate project could present their arguments at these meetings, too.

As a member of the Open Space Committee, a subcommittee of the Eternity Conservation Commission, Marion was officially opposed to the development plans of the Seatham Corporation. Seatham, a huge Boston firm with branches in Atlanta and Houston, wanted to rezone several hundred acres in Eternity so that it could slap up a clutch of condominiums overlooking the ocean, a view that would triple the asking price of each unit but, in Marion's opinion, would irrevocably ruin the pristine area.

She arrived at Town Hall with indigestion, but at least she was on time. From the back of the room she scanned the small group already seated. The Seatham Corporation's principal executives had not deigned to leave their Boston high-rise offices to make this meeting, but that didn't matter. They were more than ably represented tonight, she noted. For in the front row sat their most recently hired attorney-at-law, one Geoffrey Kent.

CHAPTER TWO

THE METAL CHAIRS were arranged in rows with a narrow aisle down the middle. Careful not to look at Geoff, Marion took a seat with the two other Open Space members who'd been delegated to show up tonight. For a few minutes, she chatted quietly with them, even while her heart was racing away. She told herself to relax. Confronting Geoff for the first time as an estranged wife would be hard, but first times were always the worst. It would become easier after this. It would.

Finally, when she could contain her curiosity no longer, she angled a look his way. He was looking back. Unexpectedly a shaft of pain cut through her. Oh, how she'd missed this man! How lonely the house had become since he'd left! She hadn't let herself admit it until this moment.

He nodded hello. Taut lines bracketed his mouth.

Marion nodded back, her eyes sweeping over him as if seeing him for the first time. She guessed separation did that to people.

He was a remarkably attractive man. Actually, "perfect" was the word she'd used at nineteen when describing him to her friend Bronwyn. But being tall, dark and handsome was only part of Geoff's appeal. Granted, it was the part women usually noticed first: the lean six-foot-one frame, solid with sinuous muscle, the long-lashed dark brown eyes and thick sun-tipped brown hair.

But within minutes of meeting him women noticed something more. Even when he was at his most reserved, Geoff simmered with an unnerving sex appeal. It came across in the usual ways: the penetrating stare, the slow half-cocked grin and loose-limbed stride. Yet Marion was well aware that his appeal ran deeper than that. His intelligence, his integrity and affable nature were every bit as seductive as his physical assets. Maybe more so.

There once had been a time when the female attention he drew used to amuse Marion and fill her with pride. Now, with that unbidden response rising within herself, she felt only disgust. How could she possibly feel anything for a man who no longer wanted her and had let her know it in the most demoralizing way?

With a start, she realized his gaze was moving over her with the same slow attention she'd just been paying him. He was probably wondering what he'd ever seen in her. Under his scrutiny she felt like a plain freckled urchin who had never quite grown up—at least not into the kind of woman who could hold the interest of a man like Geoff.

Inadvertently her mind filled with an image of Tiffany Taylor, the in-house lawyer with Seatham who'd been assisting Geoff since February—a sort of liaison between the firm and him. With her long black hair and exotic green eyes, voluptuous figure and fashionable wardrobe, Tiffany represented everything Marion felt she lacked. Not only was Tiffany physically beautiful, she was also dynamic and intelligent.

Marion was relieved to see that Tiffany wasn't here tonight. She didn't think she could have handled having to face her, too.

"Shall we get this meeting started?" The chairman of the planning board took his seat at the long table up front. Seatham was first on the agenda tonight. These days, Seatham was always first on the agenda.

Representatives of the development firm had started prowling around Eternity well over a year ago. No one seemed to notice, though, until last January when, to everyone's amazement, the Borden family let it be known they'd accepted an option-to-buy offer on their property, a 260-acre farm out near Eternity Point.

For as long as anyone could remember, the Borden place had been worked as a farm. Its acreage was diverse and beautiful. It included the high dryland where the house and barns were located, cornfields, rolling pastures that dipped to salt marsh, and almost two hundred acres of woods; and then there was the precious ocean frontage, ironically the segment that was least valuable to farmers in the past.

Marion had been stunned by the news of Seatham's move on this land, but her reaction was nothing compared to how she'd felt when Geoff came home one snowy February night and told her he'd agreed to be retained by Seatham as their town-based legal counsel. Not only was she outraged that he'd gone over to the enemy, but he hadn't even bothered to consult her.

The spring months passed in a blur of committee meetings. Understandably Seatham wouldn't buy the land until they were assured they had the town's blessing to build. That meant arguing their case to just about every board in the town—zoning, health, building, conservation. To Marion's dismay, the normally ready-to-rally citizens of Eternity remained cautiously quiet, willing to listen to Seatham's arguments—primarily because Geoffrey Kent was doing the arguing. Geoff was liked and admired and had a reputation for being honest. If *he* thought the Seatham development would be beneficial to the town, the reasoning went, then most likely it was true. At times Marion thought that Seatham had chosen Geoff precisely because of his influence.

Summer arrived and so far none of Seatham's appeals had actually won unqualified approval. Change of this magnitude came slowly. But the firm was definitely making progress. They'd met objections promptly, one after another, which, according to them, proved their goodwill and sincere intention to create a development the town would be proud of.

Only the Conservation Commission and its offshoot, the Open Space Committee, stood dead set against the Seatham development. Active and vocal, they became a major thorn in Seatham's side, especially now when the whole matter was finally coming to a head. Two weeks from Monday the citizens of Eternity would gather in the high-school auditorium at a special town meeting to vote on whether they wanted the zoning changes or not. That vote would be the definitive word on whether Seatham stayed or went.

Tonight, Geoff approached the long table where the board members sat and presented three sets of revised blueprints.

"I think you'll find that the changes conform to the objections made at the last meeting." Behind him arose a few quiet twitters of laughter—people who knew where the objections had come from.

Marion, however, didn't find anything amusing in this rivalry of theirs, and her voice was deadly serious as she said, "May we see a copy, please?" She knew Geoff wasn't amused, either.

"Certainly," he said.

She heard the impatience in his answer, saw the anger building in his eyes, even if no one else did.

She opened the blueprint across her lap and tried to concentrate. For the life of her, though, all she could think about was the wedding band she'd just glimpsed on Geoff's hand.

One of her colleagues asked a question, and that gave her focus. She asked a couple, too, but it felt like token resistance. For the most part, Seatham had met objections once again.

Fortunately neither side had anything else on their agenda, and within minutes of starting, they were done. Marion got up and turned to remind Geoff she'd see him at the house, but he was already striding toward the exit, his leather-soled shoes punishing the old wooden floor.

The town center of Eternity lay a few miles inland from the ocean, up the Sussex River. Marion had lived in or near the center all her life, and even now all she had to do to get home was drive down Bridge Street, cross the river and turn onto Water Street, a tree-shaded lane that ran parallel to the river's south bank.

The house had been a "fixer-upper" when she and Geoff bought it, but she'd immediately seen its potential. Now it was a beauty, and the land—well, they'd always known a half acre of land right on the river was priceless.

When Marion got home after the meeting, however, she felt none of the peace that usually filled her upon entering this house. She went straight to her studio to work off her frustration.

Geoff's car pulled into the driveway fifteen minutes later. She heard him open the back door, heard his keys hit the counter, his steps cross the kitchen. Such familiar sounds, as much a part of this old house as its timber creaks and pipe clanks.

As his steps approached the doorway to her studio, a bead of perspiration trickled down her side. It was one thing to face him in a crowded conference room, quite another to be alone with him again in their home. Slowly she lifted her eyes from her buffing wheel.

"Hello, Marion," he said coolly.

She nodded back. "Short meeting tonight."

"Yes. But you still managed to make it interesting." His tone was so wry it was almost acid.

She only shook her head, reluctant to get drawn into an argument about Seatham in private.

Geoff stepped into the cluttered studio and crossed to the windowed wall that overlooked the back lawn and the river flowing along at its farthest reaches. They'd added all these windows so that Marion would be able to watch their children at play while she worked. Now she told people they were to provide a view of her gardens.

Geoff turned and, unbuttoning his suit jacket, sat on a sill. "Don't stop working on my account," he drawled.

With a start she realized her buffing wheel was still whirring. The sarcasm in his voice registered, and her anger rose to meet it. "What makes you think I would?"

"Not a damned thing, Marion." His resentful gaze slid away.

She didn't want to argue about her work, either. He simply didn't understand. Her jewelry designing had always been a joy. For the past couple of years it had become her escape. As Geoff had drifted away, becoming less and less interested in her and their home, and more and more involved in his career, she'd found deepening solace here.

"I'm sorry." She shut off the power to her machinery. "You came to discuss Robyn's wedding."

He swung his head up—surprised by her apology? she wondered—and for the first time she noticed the dark circles under his eyes. The grooves on the sides of his mouth seemed to have deepened, too.

"Yes. And to get the rest of my clothes," he reminded her. He pushed away from the window, straightening to his full rangy height. "Do you mind if we talk while I'm packing?"

Seeing how eager he was to be gone, she felt an absurd heaviness settle on her heart. She got to her feet and followed him through the house and up the stairs.

Inside their bedroom, Geoff unzipped a nylon gym bag and dropped it on the floor in front of his mahogany highboy. He opened a drawer and went straight to work, pitching underwear into the open bag. Marion remained on the threshold, reluctant to enter this particular room now that he was in it.

Her gaze swept the spacious room with its original fireplace, wide pine floorboards and occasional small pane of palely tinted glass. "I don't want to live in a museum, Marion," she remembered Geoff complaining seven years earlier when they'd begun searching for a house and she had persisted in hauling him through places built in the 1700s. The irony was *he* was the one with the pedigree that reached back to the American Revolution. "Trust me," she'd replied, and he had. She hoped he'd never regretted it.

Like the eight other rooms in the house, this one contained several period pieces. But she'd softened their effect with an abundance of country crafts, cheerful fabrics and myriad whimsical touches—like the English barrister's wig, propped on the bureau, that she'd found in an antique shop and given to Geoff one Christmas.

Her eyes moved to the canopied four-poster bed piled deep with lacy pillows. That was the first piece of furniture they'd moved into this house.

With a shuddery sigh, she leaned her spine against the doorjamb and closed her eyes....

Geoff had driven her here without saying where they were going. Just picked her up at the end of the workday with the cryptic words "I've got a surprise." She remembered an early November snow dusting the ground.

"What are we doing *here?*" she'd asked, genuinely puzzled when he'd pulled to the curb in front of the white clapboard colonial they were hoping to buy. And then Geoff had pulled the keys from his coat pocket and, grinning, jiggled them until she understood. They'd been approved for a mortgage.

With a lump in her throat, she'd walked ahead of him through the gate in the white picket fence, up the brick path to the gracefully fanlighted door.

Inside, he'd lit a candle, apologizing because the electricity was disconnected. But at least there was heat, kept on so the pipes wouldn't freeze.

The previous owners had moved out weeks earlier, and the empty house echoed as Geoff and Marion had wandered through, hand in hand. Both were filled with that wondrous joy peculiar to young couples entering their first house for the first time as owners. All of life's possibilities seemed to be waiting for them here.

They'd climbed the stairs, looked in on the three front bedrooms, smiling as if those rooms, flickering in the light of the candle Geoff carried, already contained their slumbering children. And there *would* be children, they were sure, despite the miscarriage she'd suffered three months earlier. Then they'd walked slowly to the room on the rear ell that would be theirs. This room.

Geoff had opened the door—and her breath caught. In the center of the room someone had set up a bed, the very bed she'd been admiring for months but thought they couldn't afford.

It still wore the same moth-eaten canopy that the antique dealer hadn't bothered to remove, but Geoff had supplied a new mattress and fresh white linens. In the center of the bed lay their picnic hamper, its flat top serving as a table for two crystal flutes and a bottle of champagne on ice.

Geoff had lit more candles, six of them, and when the room was a sea of wavering yellow light, he lit the kindling in the fireplace. Marion, meanwhile, sat cross-legged on the bed and watched, close to tears. And when the logs had caught, he'd turned, his dark penetrating eyes glinting with more than just reflected candles....

"So, tell me about Robyn and Nate."

She snapped open her eyes at the sound of his voice. Her daydream fragmented, leaving her feeling hollow and bereft. Geoff was zipping the bulging gym bag closed.

"There isn't much else to say beyond what I've already told you. They insist on being married in the chapel, they have a four-week time frame, and we're supposed to be their attendants. Oh, and I agreed to organize the wedding and do their rings," she added hastily.

Geoff didn't say anything as he moved to the closet, but one of his eyebrows had arched. She wondered if he was thinking she'd taken on too much. She'd been wondering that herself.

Geoff slid aside the raised-panel door. His crisp shirts and suits hung just as he'd left them. "So, when are you going to tell Robyn I can't be in the wedding?"

Marion shrugged. "I don't know."

"You'd better do it soon, Marion. I'm in no mood to be in anybody's wedding right now. Furthermore, Robyn and Nate are going to need time to make other arrangements." He unhooked two summer-weight suits and fitted them into a garment bag lying on the bed.

"I realize that. It's just that I don't know *how* to tell her, Geoff. If you could see how happy she is, you'd understand."

Geoff turned back to the closet, frowning as he flicked through his shirts. Finally he paused, staring absently, his hand hooked over the clothes bar. "It's hard to believe, isn't it? Robyn getting married."

"I know." Marion stepped into the room hesitantly. "She was just a little girl when we started dating."

Geoff nodded, almost smiling. The fan of lines around his eyes drew her attention. They hadn't been there twelve years ago. "She used to follow me everywhere."

Of course she did, Marion thought, taking a seat in a Boston rocker. Robyn had had an enormous crush on him.

Geoff unhooked an armload of shirts and returned to the bed.

Marion added, "You were great with her when she was going through those difficult teen years. Maybe a little too protective at times..."

He scowled, fitting the shirts into the garment bag. "Well, I never had a kid sister." He returned to the closet for shoes.

He'd never had any sort of sister. Or a brother, for that matter. But the loneliness he carried from his youth wasn't something he talked about, and so she let it go.

"She still has a special affection for you. For both of us." Marion let her head drop back. "You can't imagine how I dread telling her about us. She's floating on cloud nine right now. Our news is going to devastate her. It's going to destroy her wedding day, too."

Geoff's movements slowed, and she sensed that the full implications were just dawning on him. He let his shoes drop and sat on the bed, his forehead puckered. "I guess I didn't think this through."

"It's going to be horrid, Geoff. The relatives congratulating her one minute and extending their sympathy to me the next. Our breakup is going to turn her wedding into a wake. And my parents..."

Geoff looked away, his face like granite. He'd never been close to his own parents, even before they'd divorced. Too wound up in their own unhappiness with each other, they'd virtually ignored him from the time he entered school. Joining her close-knit family, he'd once said, was the second-best thing that had ever happened to him. The best was meeting her.

"I really don't know what to do. I want my sister's wedding to be as beautiful as possible, a day she'll remember fondly. I don't want her associating it with... us." She sat forward. "Do you have any suggestions on how to go about this? Really, I need help here."

He rested his forearm against a bedpost and scraped his knuckles across his chin. "How about..." He paused. "How about just not telling her?" He glanced at Marion, then away.

"What are you talking about?"

"Well, for Robyn and Nate's sake, maybe... maybe we should keep our problems to ourselves and pretend we're still living together. Just for that one day," he added quickly.

Marion laughed nervously. "You've got to be joking."

He shook his head.

"But... it's crazy. It'd never work."

"Why not? The only person I've told is Graham."

"Not Freddie?"

"Of course not. And the only reason I told Graham was I thought he deserved an explanation when I turned up on his doorstep after you threw me out."

She bristled. "I didn't throw you out. We both agreed it would be best if—"

"Agreed? You threw my briefcase down the stairs and told me never to—"

"Stop!" Marion clapped her hands over her ears. She didn't want to hear repeated what she'd said that night. "You're not here for us to rehash last week's argument."

He grumbled inarticulately but finally agreed, got off the bed and went back to packing. She could tell he was still angry, though.

After a while her curiosity got the better of her. "Is that where you've been staying? At Graham's?"

"Where'd you expect?" he asked from the closet.

"I'm really kind of surprised you didn't move right in with Tiffany."

Geoff slid the closet door closed so hard it ricocheted halfway back. "I thought we weren't going to rehash last week's argument." Although his voice was controlled, his eyes shone with an anger that made Marion wish she'd kept her comment to herself.

"You're right. I'm sorry. We're fine when we're just talking about Robyn, but once—"

"Then let's stick to Robyn. Really, she's the person we should be thinking about right now."

"Yes, of course. So, where were we?"

"We were discussing who we'd told about our separation, and I said only Graham. Who have you told?"

"Only Bronwyn."

"Well, there. Two people. Seems to me that keeping our problem a secret would be a snap." He swung the garment bag over his shoulder and grabbed up the gym bag.

"I don't agree." Marion rose and followed him out to the hall.

"Why not?"

She huffed. "Do you actually believe no one else has noticed? I mean, your car hasn't been here in a week. You only had one suit. People aren't blind, Geoff. They know. At least they suspect. I've been getting some mighty strange looks lately. And by the time the wedding rolls around, the whole town will've caught on. Word is bound to reach my sister's ears."

Geoff stared into space, his frown darkening. "As much as I want to argue the point, I can't. You're right."

"Darn right I'm right." They started down the stairs. "And the problem isn't just people in town leaking word. My family will be stopping by here the day before the wedding, maybe even staying over. They're sure to notice changes, your things missing. There's no way we'd be able to pull off a convincing pretense that we're still together."

Geoff paused and turned, looking up at her. "Unless, of course..." His voice thinned.

"What?" she asked cautiously.

"Unless we really are."

Marion swallowed. Their eyes met and locked for several endless seconds.

"Don't misunderstand me," he added, blinking and glancing away. "All I'm saying is I could move back to the house just until the wedding is over."

"Of course. I didn't think you meant anything else."

"We have plenty of room," he continued. "So we wouldn't have to sl—" He stopped. "We wouldn't get in each other's way. We don't even have to talk if you don't want."

"True." Marion nodded, even as the irony struck her: they'd bought this big house hoping to fill it with children and laughter and happy noise. Instead, he was proposing they use the extra space to guarantee their distance and silence.

"So, what do you say, Marion? Should I move back in?"

She returned to reality, shaking her head. "No. It's crazy." She continued down the stairs, careful not to touch him as she passed.

"Why? You asked for my advice, and this is the only answer I can come up with. It's a damn good answer, too. Think about it, Marion." He dropped his bags at the front door. "We both want Rob and Nate to be happy and have a nice wedding. Neither of us wants to upset your parents. And if you're at all interested, I don't much care for the idea of somebody else taking my place as their best man."

She stared at his tie. She wanted to say no, had every intention of saying no—but then he lowered his head to her eye level and did the worst thing possible. He smiled. She'd always been a sucker for his smile.

"Come on," he entreated softly.

She swallowed, then swallowed again.

"For Robyn's sake."

"All right!" She threw up her hands. "All right!" she agreed, silently wishing a pox on all silver-tongued lawyers.

Geoff released a long breath. "Good. I'll go get my things at Graham's and be back in, oh, two hours."

Two? Getting his things at Graham's shouldn't take more than thirty minutes. Marion's eyes narrowed. And who else was he going to see in the meantime?

"Don't expect me to wait up," she said icily.

He laughed deep in his throat. "It's so nice to be home again."

After Geoff drove away, Marion carried the bags he'd packed up to one of the guest rooms. She finished emptying his closet and moved his toiletries from their private bath to the bathroom down the hall. All the while her sense of unease continued to grow, her sense that she'd made the wrong decision.

Considering how deeply Geoff had hurt her, how could she possibly allow him back into this house? Why was she putting herself in a position where she'd have to see him every day and be reminded that he was involved with someone else and, as soon as Robyn's wedding was over, intended to move out? A clean break would be so much easier.

Her emotional well-being wasn't the only thing she was worried about, however. With so much anger and pain between them, how would she and Geoff ever convince anyone they were still a happily married couple?

But most disturbing of all—if she and Geoff were finished, if she indeed wanted the split as much as she'd been telling herself all week, then why was she secretly rejoicing over this four-week reprieve?

One thing she had no question about. These were going to be the hardest four weeks of her life.

CHAPTER THREE

GEOFF REACHED BACK, swung his racket and slammed the ball so hard it blurred. It hit the front wall near the left corner, caromed off the side and was just a flash of blue when it spun past Graham's flailing racket.

"Son of a..." Graham Reed straightened from his crouch. "This is just a game of racquetball, pal, not a matter of life and death."

"My point," Geoff panted. He turned and waited for his best friend to toss him the retrieved ball. "That's nine four."

They were well into their third game of the night, yet, despite all the physical exertion, Geoff still felt no release of tension. He was also heading for his third straight lopsided win, but felt no sense of victory.

He dropped into his serving position and smashed the ball mercilessly, imagining it contained all the frustrations he'd been harboring for weeks—no, months, maybe more.

"Ten four," Graham muttered, the inevitability of defeat flattening his voice. He wiped his forehead with his wristband, brushing aside a damp shock of mahogany-red hair. "So, what's Marion and her Open Space group done now?"

Geoff had stepped out to the corridor and was taking a swig from his water bottle when the question caught him. He coughed. "Nothing."

"Okay. So what hasn't she done that's got you so steamed?"

"Why do you assume my every mood revolves around Marion?" he asked, stepping back into the court and closing the door.

"Because it does. It always has. And now that you two have landed on opposite sides in this Borden Farm deal, it's even worse. In a way, I guess, it's kind of funny. Well, to some people."

"What's funny?" Geoff challenged, trying to channel his anger into the ball he was steadily bouncing and catching.

"You know, you and Marion pitted against each other, like in those old screwball comedies. Spencer Tracy and Katharine Hepburn, Cary Grant and—"

"Believe me, it isn't much of a comedy when you're living it." Geoff turned and served, winning the point easily.

He and Graham had been friends for twelve years, since the summer Geoff had moved to Eternity with his newly divorced father. They'd come up from Boston, from a neighborhood that had gone from respectable working class to a war zone in just Geoff's lifetime. Out of necessity he'd grown up tough.

But he'd never seen the sense in fighting. He got good grades and had better things to do with his time. So, along with his ability to stand his ground, he'd also developed a personable nature. Street diplomacy. That rare blend of toughness, humor and integrity that won a person enough respect to be left to follow his own pursuits.

By the time he moved to Eternity he'd already finished three years of college. He hadn't considered himself young or dependent for a decade, and he'd never been insecure. That summer, though, he was lonely.

His father had a few relatives here, distant cousins and an aunt—apparently Kent roots went back a couple of hundred years—but Geoff had felt he had no one. He'd tried to tell himself it didn't matter. He was just marking time and would soon be moving on. Still, his sense of isolation and rootlessness that summer had been painful.

And then one evening he'd passed a school yard and seen a tall redheaded guy shooting baskets, alone. That evening he found a best friend.

The following week life became complete, and Geoff had never thought of leaving Eternity since. He'd found Marion then, working for the summer in her parents' jewelry store right up the street from the diner where he'd gotten a job. The moment she'd stepped into the place to pick up her parents' lunch order, Geoff had known he was lost. In fact, he'd dropped an entire carton of eggs when their eyes met.

Marion was the most beautiful girl in the world, the sweetest, the kindest—a golden princess to whom he'd pledged to be a prince for the rest of his life....

Abruptly Graham's voice brought him back to the present. "I thought you'd be happy about moving back tonight." He was slapping his racket against his palm, waiting for Geoff to serve.

"I already told you, my moving back doesn't mean a thing. I wish you'd get it out of your head that this is some sort of reconciliation." Geoff served.

"Yeah, I heard what you said." Graham lunged, flicked the ball and crashed to the floor. But at least he'd made contact. "You're only going back," he panted, pushing himself up, "for the kid sister's sake."

"Damn right." Geoff waited for Graham to get into position again. "And Marion's doing it for the same reason."

His serve this time was too easy, and Graham made a kill shot into the right corner, then raised his arms high and did a farcical victory dance.

Geoff flipped him the ball. "Believe me, Marion and I are just putting off the inevitable. I'm not about to forget she threw me out." He didn't think he'd ever forget that. "And as soon as Robyn's wedding is over—" he tried to return Graham's serve but missed "—she wants me out again. I wouldn't be surprised if she had my bags on the lawn before I even took off my tux."

They continued to play, and for a while Graham got into the game, but Geoff won by scoring the final three points.

They slumped to the floor, their backs against opposite walls.

"One more game?" Graham asked.

Geoff's only answer was to roll his head side to side.

"Good."

They continued to sit, cooling down.

"One other thing," Geoff said after a while. "All this talk about our separation and my moving back just being a pretense—this is all confidential. Okay?"

Graham looked at him awhile, frowning. "Yeah. I understand." Pensively he twirled his racket between his bent knees. "You know, I don't mean to pry," he said carefully. "We both like our privacy in certain matters...."

"And I appreciate how you've respected that. Really. I showed up at your house a week ago, told you Marion and I were having problems and I needed a place to crash, and you never asked any questions, just took me in."

"It's only what you would've done for me. But sometimes...sometimes beating up a small rubber ball doesn't work out all the demons."

Geoff agreed silently, reminded that there were maybe more demons than Graham suspected. But how could he tell even a friend as tried and true as Graham that he had begun to feel unnecessary in his wife's life? For the past couple of years she'd so immersed herself in her jewelry-making that her work had grown far beyond his ability to really appreciate it. He didn't know the words to say, didn't understand anymore what she was attempting in her art. And the harder he tried to find words that meant the same as "nice" but were bigger, more suitable, the more he seemed to fail in communicating his interest.

What really bothered him, though, was that other people had entered her life who did speak her language. She'd joined an artisans' co-op a couple of years back, and it seemed her life had done a one-eighty overnight. The co-op store provided a new showcase for her work, and some of the more experienced members introduced her to even better markets—pricey catalogs, galleries on Boston's Newbury Street....

Marion was one talented lady, all right, and he couldn't help wondering where her career would be now if she'd gotten right to it after they were married. Instead, she'd worked all day in her parents' store to help him finish law school, leaving her designing to whatever free hours she could find at night or on weekends.

Lord, she didn't even finish college. They'd been so tired of dating long-distance, so impatient to be together, that, with only one year left at Rhode Island School of Design, she'd insisted on dropping out to marry him.

And then there were all those years when every waking thought seemed directed toward having a baby. Now she was working so obsessively that Geoff suspected she was trying to make up for lost time. Not only did he feel unnecessary in her life, he also felt resented, and he didn't have a doubt she was just using the incident with Tiffany as an excuse to get out of their marriage.

Geoff was able to understand the work Marion did with the Open Space Committee a little better than he understood her jewelry-making, although her joining a committee had come as something of a surprise. She'd always loved the town, loved the area, and had often volunteered to assist at the recycling station or plant flowers somewhere or clean storm debris from the river. But her help had always been quiet, physical, in-the-background sort of work.

When he was hired by Seatham, he wasn't aware she'd gotten so involved in policy-making, and he certainly hadn't thought it would cause another crisis in their relationship.

As he saw it, the Borden property had merely been a farm, a working farm, and as such, no one really got to go there except friends of the Bordens. With condos on it, many more people would be able to appreciate the view and enjoy the land. Geoff even liked the building designs Seatham had come up with. So, when Marion told him the Open Space Committee was going to oppose Seatham, he'd been stunned. He had never imagined anyone in town would protest Seatham's plans, least of all his wife.

Graham had said people thought their taking opposite sides was comical. Well, he sure as hell hadn't laughed when she'd dropped that bomb on him.

It had been bad enough they'd had all that trouble trying to have a child. Then Marion had jumped into her work so deeply he didn't feel he was a part of her life anymore. And finally this. She'd taken hold of the one thing he felt he was really good at—the law—and opposed him at a crucial juncture of his professional life. Comic? What the hell was funny about that?

Actually it was pretty pathetic. He'd come home with the news that he'd signed on with Seatham thinking Marion would be pleased, maybe even impressed. Seatham was the biggest client he'd ever had. It only went to prove how little he knew the woman he'd married, how far apart they'd grown.

There were at least five minutes left before the next twosome was due to take the court, but Graham got stiffly to his feet and started heading for the door. Geoff followed, picked up his towel and water bottle in the carpeted corridor and trailed his friend to the locker room.

Twenty minutes later they were sitting at the food bar in the lounge. New Age music and conversation swirled around them. Geoff ordered a club sandwich, fries and diet soda. Graham got a small basket of nachos.

"It's almost ten o'clock, pal," Graham said. "Don't you ever eat on time anymore?"

"Six o'clock, ten o'clock, what's the difference as long as I eat?"

"Boy, I'm glad you're going home." Graham shook his head. "So, have you calmed down enough to talk about it? Or would you rather listen to how much fun I had drilling teeth today?"

Geoff smiled, appreciating how Graham hadn't pressed the issue back at the court and had let him cool off quietly. But maybe there was some point in explaining what had happened. Maybe a more objective view would help.

"Okay. Here it is," he said after a moment's thought. "Marion and I haven't been doing too well lately, especially with this Seatham deal between us. But the thing that finally set us off was really strange, something I never would've figured."

"Tiffany Taylor?"

"What? How did you know?"

"I may appear to be a mild-mannered dentist, but I'm really an expert on the human heart—especially the female heart. And that Tiffany, well, I always thought she looked a little too interested in you, and the two of you working together was going to cause trouble."

Their food arrived, but Geoff only stared at his plate. "No, it wasn't like that. Well," he hedged, "when we first started working together, I did get the feeling she wouldn't have minded if something happened between us. But I made it perfectly clear I wasn't interested, and after that I never had any problems with her. None. She's been great. But this one night... it was strange." He frowned, taking a bite of his sandwich. "Tiff and I had been working in my office. It was late, but not very. We were almost ready to knock it off when, I can't remember why exactly, she asked me to clarify some idea I'd come up with the day before. Then, when I'd explained it, she said something like, 'Oh, of course! That's perfect!' and threw her arms around me. It was a hug, that's all. And a kiss, but more on the side of my mouth, you know? Not right on the lips. Her reaction surprised me a little because I hadn't thought the suggestion I'd made was that much of a breakthrough. But then I was *really* surprised because I saw Marion standing in the doorway, and she looked so mad I thought she was going to shoot us both."

Graham swore quietly. "That poor kid."

"I know. She apologized over and over—"

"Not Tiffany." Graham turned, incredulous. "I'm talking about your wife. Walking in on a scene like that..." He shook his head.

Geoff's stomach clenched defensively. "It wasn't 'a scene like that.' It was all perfectly innocent, but before anybody could say a word, Marion took off."

"I hope you followed her."

"Of course I followed her. I could see she'd misunderstood."

"Had she?" Graham asked pointedly.

"What do you mean, had she?"

"Well, are you sure she didn't see exactly what Tiffany wanted her to see?"

Geoff drummed his fingers in a tight staccato. "You have a suspicious mind, Reed."

"Maybe. But from the first time I met her, I've always thought Tiffany was too shrewd and conniving for anybody's good."

"You've got it all wrong. It was Marion, Marion who blew the incident out of proportion." Geoff sighed in frustration. "I tried to explain to her nothing was going on, I really did. But she wouldn't listen. After all we've been through, you'd think she'd at least do that. But the truth is, Marion didn't *want* to listen. She sees Tiffany as a ticket out of our marriage. That's why she pounced on the incident and wouldn't let it go."

Graham looked skeptical. "You're sure of that?"

"Yes. Her behavior doesn't make sense otherwise, all that insisting I was having some sort of affair when there's never been anything between me and Tiff except a friendship and a mutual respect." He paused. "You know, she's really a good lawyer."

"She's really a gorgeous one, too, pal," Graham added. Geoff didn't like his narrowed stare. Was Graham's suspicious mind now questioning *his* motives?

"Okay. She is. But there are lots of pretty women in the world. From the first time I saw Marion, every other woman has been just—a woman. The pretty ones, the not-so-pretty ones, it hasn't mattered. Marion's the only woman I ever wanted."

"Even now?"

Geoff picked up his sandwich and took a desultory bite.

"Even now?" Graham persisted.

"Now Marion doesn't seem to want me. She's got her store and her jewelry-making, new friends and committees, so what I want or don't want doesn't really matter, does it?"

Graham must have heard the edge in his voice. He chomped on a nacho, looked toward the TV behind the bar and said, "How about those Red Sox? Some season they're having, huh?"

THE FIRST THING on Marion's mind when she opened her eyes the next morning was Geoff. Was he still in the house? Where? And could she get up and go about her routine without bumping into him?

She glanced at the clock and shot to a sitting position. Good Lord, it was already nine-fifteen! Usually she was up and working in her studio by eight. But then, she hadn't slept very well last night, had she?

She'd made sure she was in bed before Geoff got home. She'd had no desire to face him after he'd spent the evening with Tiffany. She'd heard him enter by the kitchen, heard him open the refrigerator, imagined him having a drink, then walking into his study.

A short time later he'd climbed the stairs, quietly, slowly. She'd lain very still, listening. And then she'd stiffened. Instead of turning into the guest room, his footsteps had continued up the dark hall, coming to a halt outside her door. She'd stopped breathing.

Did he call her name? She wasn't sure. Should she answer? She didn't so much as blink, her eyes wide with unreasoning fear, though why she was frightened was beyond her. The next moment, his steps retreated, and she surmised he'd merely made a mistake, come to their bedroom out of habit. She'd heard the door to the guest room close, but it had been hours before sleep finally released her from her troubled thoughts.

Now she got out of bed and tiptoed down the hall to the room he'd occupied. Peeking in, she noticed the bed was neatly made. She crossed the room and looked out the window to where he usually parked his car. It was gone.

She slumped with relief. Which was absurd, she told herself. They'd shared the same house for ten years. Why the tension now? Why this sense of walking on eggs?

But of course she knew why. Things weren't the same as they'd been ten years ago, or five, or even two weeks ago.

She and Geoff had entered into something brand-new, this living together while waiting to separate, and she wasn't at all sure she knew the rules. She wasn't even sure there *were* rules.

Certainly this heightened sensitivity she'd acquired toward him made little sense. In fact, it was ludicrous that being in this room where he'd slept should hold such a curious edge of excitement. You'd think she was trespassing.

Yesterday's shirt was hooked on a bedpost. She stared at it a moment, then picked it off, intending to take it to the hamper. Instead she held the shirt out, imagining Geoff's strong shoulders filling it. Slowly she pressed the shirt to her cheek. The fragrance of his soap still lingered in the smooth cotton folds. She swallowed, detecting also the faint but distinctive scent of his skin.

Abruptly she tossed the shirt back and spun away. What she was perceiving was probably just Tiffany's perfume. Besides, she had to concentrate on Robyn's wedding today, at least for a couple of hours. She hurried from the room, shut the door firmly behind her and headed for the shower.

An hour later, Marion arrived at the Powell estate, eager to book a date for her sister's wedding. She found Bronwyn in the Powell Museum, a small local archive housed in a back wing of the mansion. She was kneeling on the carpet in her office, slicing open a cardboard carton, one of several stacked about the room. The sun streaming in the window turned her ash-blond hair nearly white.

"Looks like Christmas morning in here."

Bronwyn glanced up and smiled. "Marion! Hi!" She pushed aside some wood shavings and lifted out a delicate porcelain figurine, part of the museum's latest bequest.

"More China Trade loot?"

"Mm. Isn't this gorgeous? Have a seat." She lay the figurine back in its box and settled more comfortably on the rug. "What brings you here this time of day?"

"Are you ready for the big news? Robyn and Nate are getting married."

Bronwyn let out a gasp. "Your baby sister?"

"My reaction exactly."

"When? Give me all the details."

"There are no details yet. Everything hinges on whether we can book a date with you."

"Well, of course you can book a date with me. What month?"

Marion chuckled. "This month."

"*This* month?"

"Well, within four weeks, which'll just take us into July."

"You're joking. You are, aren't you?"

"I wish." Marion then took a few minutes to explain the predicament.

Before she finished, Bronwyn was already shaking her head. "Without even looking at my calendar I can tell you I'm swamped that weekend. Are you sure they can't make it the next?"

"Positive. Nate will already be at his new station."

"Well, let's see what I have." Bronwyn got to her feet. "You know, the toughest job you're facing at this late date is finding a place for the reception." She reached across her desk for her appointment book.

"I don't suppose the house is available?" Marion asked, referring to the Powell mansion. Bronwyn's aunts, who owned the estate, had recently caught the Weddings, Inc. spirit and begun offering its beautiful grounds for garden receptions.

"Not a chance. We're booked solid into September." She opened the book. "I assume you're shooting for the Saturday?"

"Definitely. You know how hard Friday and Sunday ceremonies are on travelers. And frankly, I really don't care for them. When it comes to weddings, I'm an unabashed traditionalist. Holy mackerel! You have two ceremonies Friday evening. I couldn't book a time with you then even if I wanted to."

"And take a look at Saturday. Five weddings, Marion."

"Five?"

"Uh-huh. Ten o'clock, eleven, twelve, one and two. The two o'clock is having their reception here. That's why I've made that the last ceremony of the day. I refuse to officiate over a marriage with music and revelry in the background."

"Hmm. And I really think nine in the morning is too early. Oh, Bron! What am I going to do?"

Bronwyn flipped back a page. "Aha!"

"'Aha' what?"

"How about the week before?"

"You mean three weeks from now?"

"Yes. Last Saturday in June I have a twelve and a two slot open."

"*Three* weeks?" Marion repeated faintly.

"Uh-huh."

"How the devil can I pull together a wedding in three weeks?"

"Same way you'd pull one together in four. Both time frames are pretty impossible. But situations like this are one of the reasons we formed Weddings, Inc., remember?"

Marion groaned, pressing a hand to her somersaulting stomach. "I don't need this."

For a long while they stood at the desk, staring at the unyielding appointment book. Finally Marion sighed.

"Let's give Robyn a call and see what she thinks."

Naturally, Robyn thought the date was wonderful. Head over heels in love, she found everything wonderful these days. When Marion got off the phone, she was laughing in spite of herself.

"Were you able to follow our conversation?"

"Pretty much. I gather she wants the two-o'clock slot. And she's already bought her invitations?"

"Yes. The card-shop kind where you simply fill in the blanks. She claims they'll be in the mail tomorrow."

"Many people?"

"Between fifty and sixty. She asked if I'd check into reception sites, too, and I'm not to let cost affect my choice, she said. She called our parents last night, and they insist on picking up the tab."

"As if there was any doubt." Bronwyn pushed aside a stack of art magazines and sat on her desk. "Your parents got such a kick out of marrying you off. What an affair that was."

"Sure, but they had nearly a year to plan it."

An uneasy quiet settled between them.

"Are things any better with you and Geoff these days?" Concern darkened Bronwyn's eyes.

Marion's stomach clenched. "Well, he's...moved back."

Bronwyn popped off the desk and shrieked triumphantly, a most uncharacteristic sound coming from her. "I knew it! I just knew you two would get back together."

"No, no, it isn't like that. It's just until my sister's wedding. Geoff and I both think it would be kinder not to upset my parents or spoil Robyn's big day with our troubles. I'm going to wait till later to tell them, much later. By then Geoff'll be long gone."

But Bronwyn remained unconvinced. "I don't care what you say. You two are going to get back together."

Marion stared at her, incredulous. Hadn't she been listening?

"You were married in the Eternity Chapel," Bronwyn reminded her. "Or have you forgotten that fact?"

Marion studied her friend's blithe smile and, out of nowhere, began shaking with exasperation. "I've had it up to here with the chapel legend." Her hand cut across her eyebrows. "If I never hear another word about it, that won't be too soon for me."

"But—"

"No buts. Aside from Geoff, you're the most clearheaded, intelligent person I know, but in this matter you've always had a blind spot. When you talk about the chapel, you become so..." Words like "naive" and "shallow" flashed through her mind. "You become so irrational you drive me batty." Marion rose from her chair and paced, trying not to notice Bronwyn's pained expression. "Bron, *think* a minute. Use reason," she implored. "How long have people been coming to the chapel to be married?"

"Oh, more than a hundred years."

"Right. And in all that time do you really believe that not one of those couples has separated or had an unhappy marriage? Given the numbers, not *one?*"

Bronwyn's lips parted, but apparently she was too stunned to speak.

"I refuse to believe that Geoff and I are the first." Marion also refused to take on the responsibility. No one could bear that much weight.

"My conviction about you and Geoff isn't based only on the legend, Marion. I've never known a couple who were more right for each other."

Marion fixed her stinging eyes on a point outside the window. "Could've fooled me."

"You can't still be worried over that... that Tiffany."

Usually Marion didn't indulge in coffee-klatch conversations where personal matters were discussed. Talking about the inner workings of her marriage to an outsider, even a friend as close as Bronwyn, had always seemed rather like a betrayal. Yet, the previous week she'd needed to turn to someone in her emotional devastation, and turning to Bronwyn, she'd divulged the scene she'd walked in on in Geoff's office.

"That Tiffany," she now replied, "happens to be a lawyer, Bron. She's sharp, she's gorgeous and she's crazy about my husband."

"She's nothing but nail polish and hair spray in a five-hundred-dollar suit. Geoff could never be interested in her. In anybody else, for that matter. He's always been completely devoted to you."

"Yeah, right," Marion muttered sullenly, staring out the window again.

Bronwyn was quiet a moment. Then, "I know what you told me, but I still don't understand how you jumped to the brilliant conclusion he's having an affair."

Marion shrugged. "A wife knows."

"How? You've got to me more specific."

Marion sighed. She wasn't sure she was able to do that; her suspicions were so vague. Still, they'd been building all spring, one on another, until now they seemed a mountain of evidence.

Take, for instance, that picture in the town newspaper, shot six weeks ago at a meeting of the board of selectmen. Ostensibly the photo was of Geoff, about to make a point, but Tiffany was sitting next to him and he'd leaned in to hear something she'd whispered. There was the slightest trace of a smile beginning on his lips, a sparkle of...of something in his eyes. He was looking toward the board, but really all his attention was fixed on the woman whispering in his ear, the woman whose fingertips with their long painted nails rested on his upper arm.

It was the intimation of intimacy that had gotten to Marion, the image of a beautiful young woman whispering to a powerful and handsome man. The leaning in. The hand on the suited bicep. But more than that, it was the fact that Tiffany *did* have his ear, that they'd been working so closely that he *did* trust her and value whatever she was saying.

But how could Marion convey what that picture said to her? Bronwyn would laugh and probably call her paranoid.

There had been other things, too. Lipstick on one of his handkerchiefs. Phone calls late at night when, if she answered, the caller hung up. A hotel in New York phoning to confirm a reservation Geoff had made—for two. Of course when Geoff had called back, he'd clarified he would be the room's only occupant, but by then Marion had grown so uncertain of what was happening in her world, she'd been more than ready to believe he was lying.

"There, see?" Bronwyn said. "I didn't think you could come up with any hard evidence if you really thought about it."

Marion was losing patience. "For heaven's sake, Bronwyn, wake up! They're always together. They've taken overnight trips...."

"I still don't believe it. Not Geoff."

Marion gave up. With a long sigh, she explained, "It didn't just happen out of the blue. We've been drifting apart for about two years. But I suppose it was inevitable. We're basically just too dissimilar."

"Dissimilar? I'm not sure I understand. True, your work is different, but does that really matter?"

"Well, of course it does. Our work is who we are. It determines the people we associate with. It's what drives us. It even affects how we dress."

"Marion, don't you think you're putting a bit too much importance on what you do for a living?"

"No, I don't!" She paused with her steepled hands pressed to her lips. "What I'm trying to say is, our work is an outgrowth of our temperaments, and in that sense it's extremely important. For instance, I've always preferred working by myself. I'd rather handle things than people—metal, tools, flowers. I'm better with them."

"So?"

"So then there's Geoff, the consummate people person. He's brilliant with people. He's brilliant *period,* and his looks don't hurt, either. People are just naturally drawn to him, and I..." She hesitated, spreading her hands in a gesture of helplessness. "I can't keep up with him. I can't keep up." She turned back to the window, refusing to allow tears to surface. "I don't belong in his life anymore. I don't think I ever did."

"Nonsense. Those differences were always there, but they never stopped you two from being close in the past. I mean, you used to be so involved in each other's lives a person could barely tell the two of you apart. You even used to finish sentences for one another. Believe me, it wasn't fun listening. All that head turning gave a person whiplash."

Marion frowned. "Sexual attraction, that's all it was. Hormones. We were barely out of our teens when we got married. What did we know? For a while we put our individuality on hold, but as time went on..." She lowered her eyes. "All I know is, one day I woke up and realized Geoff was spending very little time with me and lots with other people. I guess he'd reached the point where he couldn't ignore our differences anymore and he'd gone off and found people on his level, people who thought the way he did, who had the same interests, people who didn't bore him." She swallowed with difficulty.

"People like Tiffany?"

"Exactly like Tiffany."

"I'm sorry, but I'm still not ready to buy that."

Marion could see she was getting nowhere. "Why are you taking his side?" she asked irritably. "You're my friend. You should be outraged at what he did to me."

"Sorry, but I'm going to stay neutral on this one, Marion. I've known both of you too long and, well, there are usually two sides to every story."

Marion's temples pounded. "What do you mean?"

"Geoff isn't the only one who started spending more time at his work a couple of years ago. You got pretty busy yourself. It was like you and Geoff both were hell-bent on running in opposite directions." She looked up, pinning Marion with her clear green eyes. "And I can only wonder why."

The silence deepened painfully.

"What are you talking about?" Marion's voice was nearly a whisper.

Bronwyn sighed, slowly rubbing her palms together. "You and Geoff had an awful time trying to have a baby, and I often wonder if—"

Marion interrupted her with a scornful laugh. "You think our present problems are a result of our not being able to have kids? Get real."

"Think about it, Marion. Two miscarriages. The operation. All those tedious procedures down at the infertility clinic. Don't get me wrong—you and Geoff were great. You stayed cheerful through the whole ordeal. But let's face it, it had to take an emotional toll, maybe greater than you thought."

"You don't know what you're talking about." Marion's lips were so tight she could barely form the words.

"Maybe not. Why don't you tell me, then? After five years of trying to have a baby and failing, what shape was your ego in, Marion? After five years of trying to get pregnant under close medical supervision, how were you and Geoff getting along?"

Marion stared at her friend, her heart pounding. "It's none of your damn business!" She grabbed up her purse and headed toward the door. "You have no right to try and analyze my life. It's all pop psych and hot air, just as empty as your dumb chapel legend."

Bronwyn didn't move, but Marion could tell she was wounded. Too bad. Her personal life was nobody's business.

"I have only one other question," Bronwyn said quietly.

Marion stubbornly looked aside.

"Have you and Geoff considered counseling?"

Marion couldn't help laughing again. "You really don't understand, do you? It's too late for counseling."

"Don't say that. It's never—" Seeing Marion reach for the doorknob, Bronwyn added hastily, "I really think you and Geoff ought to examine that time you were trying to have a baby."

"Stop. Just stop. You don't have any idea how frustrating it is to hear this mindless pie-in-the-sky stuff about a situation that has no hope."

"There's always—"

"No. Not anymore. Geoff and I are finished, Bronwyn." Her voice, steady until now, finally broke, and the rest was merely a wobbly whisper. "All the magic has died out of our marriage."

At last Bronwyn fell silent.

Marion opened the door. "I've got to run." She stepped outside and hurried to her truck, never once looking back.

CHAPTER FOUR

GEOFF STOOD in the driveway of the Borden farm, staring at the Seatham vice president who'd flown up from Atlanta ostensibly to tour the property. But from the start Geoff could sense something else was on O'Toole's mind.

"You want me to what?"

"Come to work for Seatham full-time. Be one of our in-house attorneys. Like Tiffany."

Geoff leaned against the sun-warmed fender of his car and crossed his arms. "I've already got a good practice."

The executive then quoted a salary that momentarily winded him, although he remained as poker-faced as he could.

"What exactly would I have to do to earn that sort of money?"

"Same thing you're doing for us now, basically. Except—" O'Toole smiled "—you'd be doing it in California."

Geoff stood away from his car as if it had zapped him with electricity. "California?"

"That's right. Seatham's looking at a two-hundred-acre parcel of land near Carmel too sweet to describe. You'd be working as part of our legal team on the whole deal, from acquisition to unloading."

"How long's that?"

"Two, maybe three years. I know it's a big decision. You'll need to think about it, talk to your wife."

"When do you need an answer?"

"No rush. Three weeks."

"For a move that big, that sounds pretty rushed to me."

"Well, that's because we'd really like you out there and working a month from now. I know that leaves a lot of loose ends here, like what to do with your house, but we'll make it worth your while, believe me. And to help you make up your mind, we're going to fly you out there for a few days."

Geoff's right eyebrow arched. He didn't like other people orchestrating his life.

"If you can clear your calendar, that is. We've got a couple of problems we need you to start looking into, but mostly you'd just be meeting the other Seatham people there, maybe local officials. You'd still have plenty of time to take off, drive around, soak up the atmosphere. I know you're going to love the area."

Geoff shoved his hands in his trouser pockets and rocked on the soles of his shoes. He couldn't believe he was actually considering the offer, but it did have appeal. The money was phenomenal. The work was new and challenging. And California? Well, it was somewhere to go and lose himself after his marriage ended.

"What happens when that project's done two or three years down the road?"

"I was hoping you'd ask." The executive grinned. "We should be breaking ground for Seatham Seattle, our new West Coast branch, some time this winter. When it's done we'd sure like it if you'd let us put your name on one of its doors."

"Your offering me a permanent position on the West Coast?"

"That's right. But you don't have to give us a decision about that for, oh gosh, a year."

Geoff's eyes narrowed. "I have to ask you something. Why me?"

"Why not you?"

Geoff shook his head. "That's not good enough."

O'Toole shrugged. "Okay. I'll admit at first we hired you because we wanted a man in this town who knew the locals and had their respect. But it didn't take long before we realized we'd taken on one helluva lawyer. Ms. Taylor was the first to notice."

"Tiffany?"

"Yes. She's the one who suggested we look more closely at you, and we did. We really liked what we saw."

Geoff was still bothered by several questions, but at that moment a pickup truck came barreling up the road and his attention shifted. He was standing on a rise at the top of the Borden farm's long driveway, with enough open field between him and the road to see the pickup skittering around the curve a quarter mile away. He shaded his eyes, hoping the sun had affected his vision. But no, it was Marion all right. That small jutting chin, that long blond hair whipping out the window—he'd know her from twice the distance. She zoomed by and was gone in seconds.

Geoff brought the conversation with the Seatham vice president to a close as soon as was politely possible, then threw himself behind the wheel of his car and sped off in the direction Marion had gone. He had a hunch where she was headed, and when he got there he was going to wring her reckless little neck.

AT THE END of Lafayette Road stood the entrance to the town beach. The attendant at the gate checked Marion's resident sticker and waved her through.

But instead of driving toward the crowded parking lot ahead, she took a dirt road to the left marked Mattasquamicutt Hill. The road climbed halfway up an egg-shaped drumlin, then fanned out to form a small parking area. After locking her truck and ramming her sun hat on her head, Marion started up a walking path.

She was puffing when she reached the top of the hill, but the climb had been worth it. Its 360-degree view was breathtaking. From where she stood, Marion could gaze outward to the boundless Atlantic, silvery with sunlight, or look down on sunbathers at the town's five-mile-long beach. Turning to the right, she could see the thousands of acres of dunes that backed the beach, with their fragile grasses and tough low pines. And turning more, she could see inland, fifty miles if the day was clear.

She could follow the Sussex River winding its way from the lighthouse on the point through vast expanses of clam flats and salt marshes, then disappearing when the woods grew too dense. But Marion's knowing eye continued along its course, anyway, past her own house and on through Eternity.

With a flick of an eye, Marion could also take in the Borden farm. She quickly turned to face the ocean again, having no room in her heart for the troubled emotions the farm usually roused.

At one end of the otherwise grassy hilltop rose a cluster of boulders that formed a pleasant place to sit. Marion walked over, the brisk breeze tossing her hair and ruffling her loose-fitting dress. Sitting, she lifted her head and tried to pull in a deep lungful of the fresh salty air. Oddly her throat tightened up. She slumped in dejection.

What on earth had possessed her to hurt the kindest person she knew? Despite the fact that Bronwyn had touched on a sensitive subject, she shouldn't have responded with such hostility.

Marion looped her arms around her knees and gazed toward the sail-specked horizon, recalling the awful things she'd said about the chapel.

Although she no longer believed in the legend herself, why had she tried to disillusion Bronwyn, too? The chapel was so much a part of Bronwyn's heritage, the ceremonies she performed there such an integral part of her career.

Marion shut her eyes. Hot tears squeezed through her lashes. But these tears were not just for hurting the dearest friend she had. They were for herself, for Geoff and for the marriage they'd entered with such high expectations. "Things weren't supposed to turn out this way," she whispered bitterly.

Where *had* the magic gone? she wondered. How could something as wonderful as what they'd had possibly die?

Until now Marion had pointed the finger of blame in every direction but the one she instinctively knew was at the core of their problems—their inability to have children. Too much pain lay in that direction, and maybe that was why she'd reacted so vehemently when Bronwyn broached the subject.

Marion fixed her stare on the sun-dazzled waves. Gradually the world bleached out and her vision drew inward.

She and Geoff hadn't even tried to have children the first couple of years of their marriage. Blissful though they were, they'd realized they were too busy and too poor to fit a child into their lives.

But after Geoff passed the bar, the hard times seemed to be behind them. Marion cut back her hours at the store, became selective about the crafts fairs she traveled to, and they turned their thoughts to starting a family.

She told Geoff she was pregnant on their third anniversary. They were both elated. There had never been a time when they hadn't envisioned children in their lives. Several children. Even when they'd been dating, they'd talked about it.

Marion had felt especially pleased for another reason. Although Geoff claimed that his heritage didn't matter to him, carrying on a name as old as his had to have been important.

Moreover, she wanted to give him a family he could call his own. With his father recently passed away and his mother remarried, he had no one, really, but her.

Unfortunately their joy ended a few weeks later when she miscarried. Nevertheless, they took the mishap in stride. As her doctor assured them, they were young and had time. They even went ahead and bought their house.

But after another miscarriage five months later, they began to suspect that something was seriously wrong. A visit to a special clinic in Boston confirmed that she had endometriosis, a disease that often results in infertility.

Thus began an ordeal neither of them had anticipated when they'd spoken the words "For better or for worse." It started with surgery, a procedure her doctor assured them would solve the problem. But when a year went by and she still failed to become pregnant, Marion began to quietly panic. Something else had to be wrong.

She and Geoff were tested, and again Marion was found to be the guilty party. Her egg production was so low and sporadic that the chances of conception, while still existent, were very slim.

Still, they remained hopeful. After all, science had devised all sorts of miraculous drugs and procedures to help couples like them achieve their dreams, and the world's best technology was only a few miles away, in Boston.

But it wasn't easy and it wasn't cheap, and eventually they reached a point where they couldn't go on.

Claiming the reasons were financial, she told her doctor to cancel their appointments in Boston until further notice, but all along she knew she and Geoff had just wanted to stop. They'd given up hope. She didn't remember them ever actually saying the words, but she knew. They'd both let go of the dream.

Marion squinted up at the sun through her wet lashes. Since then, they'd drifted apart slowly but inexorably. Not that they argued. On the contrary, they came and went in a polite routine, kept the bills paid and the house running. Yet they never really seemed to be there, even when they made love. Slowly and inexorably… One evening the TV went on during dinner, the next they went to bed at different hours, and before long they were facing each other on opposites sides of the Borden-farm issue without knowing how they'd gotten there.

But not knowing how wasn't the same as not knowing why. Marion knew why. Geoff had lost interest in her. She'd been part of a total package, a vision that included children, and once he'd realized that children weren't possible, he'd had no further use for her. She alone simply wasn't enough.

Not that he was consciously aware of thinking this way. If presented with the idea, she was sure he'd deny it soundly.

But the fact remained that for five years their existence had focused primarily on one goal—conceiving a child—and on some obscure level, Marion felt, Geoff must have come to associate her worth with becoming pregnant. When she'd failed, he'd lost interest. The magic had died, and he'd gone looking elsewhere for fulfillment.

As devastated as she was, Marion didn't blame him. Every man wanted to have his own children. That was part of living life to its fullest. Geoff was still young and virile, and there were lots of women available who could give him what he wanted and deserved. Women like Tiffany.

"Marion!" an angry male voice called. "Hey!"

She swiveled around, startled. "Geoffrey?"

He was charging across the top of the hill toward her, his sports jacket open, tie flapping, jaw set hard as steel.

Oh, Lord, and here she was with a lump in her throat so big she couldn't even talk.

"WHAT THE HELL is the matter with you?" Geoff demanded, coming to a stop directly in front of her.

She tipped her head back to look up at him. She had to squint because of the sun. "What do you mean?"

"I was down at the Borden farm just now and saw you come flying by. You must've been doing sixty, sixty-five. The speed limit on that road is forty."

She looked away, her lips tightening. "So? Did you come up here to give me a speeding ticket?"

Geoff stared at her, puzzled. Her voice was too thin for the defiant words she spoke.

"Well?" she prodded.

He blinked. "Well, what?"

"Why are you here, Geoffrey?"

He opened his mouth, then closed it. For the life of him, he couldn't come up with a reason that held water. "You were driving recklessly," he said, much of his bluster gone, "and I just wanted to let you know in case you weren't aware of the fact—though how you could be unaware is beyond me." He pushed aside his jacket and, planting his hands low on his hips, stared down at her. What was the matter with her? She kept swallowing and wetting her lips.

"For your information I was only going forty-five." She didn't look at him.

"You don't have a clue how fast you were going."

"Whether I do or don't, I can't see how it's any concern of yours. I pay the insurance on the truck. If I crack it up, it won't be any skin off your nose."

Geoff raked a hand through his hair. "Hey, knock it off. Talk like that doesn't make sense." Suddenly he knew why he'd come racing up here. Fear. Caring. A wanting to know she was safe.

"Sorry," she drawled. "I didn't mean to offend you. Why don't you hike back down and find somebody who does make sense."

Geoff let out a long slow breath. "Sounds like a good suggestion." But instead of walking away, he sat down beside her; he wasn't sure why. She didn't tell him to leave, and he wasn't sure of the reason for that, either.

"I'd forgotten the view from up here. It's really something, isn't it?"

"Yes, it is," she said.

"Mattasquamicutt. Place that sees forever," he murmured. That was the rough translation of the old Indian place name that townspeople in the nineteenth century had loosely translated to "Eternity."

Marion turned her lambent eyes on him. He'd forgotten how blue they could be. "Some people say this was a place where Indian sachems came to seek wisdom when they were troubled. 'Place that sees *into* forever' is their translation."

"I like that." He nodded, smiling a little, letting his gaze travel over her. She was wearing a soft yellow dress and a straw hat with a big cabbage rose in front. Very summery. Her hair streamed around her face and over her shoulders like a glistening sheet of honey-gold silk, and for one brief moment, he let himself remember its faintly vanilla scent, the feel of it against his lips. When was the last time he'd dipped his fingers into that glorious river of silk? And had that been, without his even knowing it, the very last time he'd get to do that?

His gaze moved to her face. She'd always had the freshest skin, with just the lightest sprinkling of freckles, skin so clear, so healthy and glowing that makeup was a travesty. Today, however, she looked tired. But then, he didn't look all that dynamic, either. For more than a week he'd been plagued with insomnia.

He glanced away sharply. "So, what particular bit of trouble brings you up here today?" he asked her, fixing his eyes on a sailboat far out on the water.

She exhaled slowly and tightened her arms around her knees. It was a while before she said, "I was just at Bronwyn's to book the chapel for Robyn's wedding, and the only date she had open is three weeks tomorrow."

"What's the matter with that?"

"What's the matter! Geoff, three weeks. That doesn't give us much time."

Her phrasing struck an unpleasant chord. Although she was clearly referring to the wedding, Geoff couldn't help thinking that three weeks was all the time left to them before they parted for good. He supposed that was the reason he was so aware of her these days. It was like when he was a kid, how he'd savored the last few days of summer, knowing vacation was coming to an end, school about to start.

"You realize Rob and Nate could simply drive up here and have a ceremony in the chapel without all the hoopla."

"I know, and she says she isn't fussy. But I also know she's always wanted a wedding with all the traditional trimmings."

"Can't Bronwyn help? That business she started..."

"Weddings, Inc.?"

"Yes. Can't she pull the wedding together for you?"

Marion unfolded from her position and stood up. "Maybe. Though she's awfully busy these days and, well, people have been organizing weddings for centuries on their own. I'm sure I'll muddle through somehow."

"So, that's what drove you up here?"

Marion walked a few paces away. "Isn't that enough?"

Knowing Marion, he didn't think so, but kept the thought to himself. He got off the stone and followed her. She was gazing down on the Borden farm.

"What were you doing over at the farm?" She held on to her hat with one had, her slender upraised arm gilded with sunlight.

"Suspicious, Marion?"

"Of course. It's my job to be."

"Don't worry, I wasn't plotting any new strategies against you and your cohorts. A Seatham exec flew up from Atlanta to look the place over and I played tour guide, that's all. It was a nonevent, really. Except—" Geoff stopped abruptly. Should he tell her about the California job offer?

No, best not to. He didn't know what he intended to do about it himself. So much depended on what *she* decided to do.

"Except what?" she asked.

"Except...I'll probably be having dinner with him tonight." Inwardly Geoff groaned. O'Toole was staying in Boston and would be meeting up with Tiffany for dinner. Now he'd have to eat out, alone, when he'd really been looking forward to going home. Maybe he'd stop by Graham's.

"I don't know, Geoffrey," Marion said disparagingly, shaking her head.

"What don't you know?"

"How you could work for that firm."

"Oh, I see. It's back to that again." Geoff felt his neck muscles tense. "You want to know what happened to my principles, where I went astray."

"Well, look at that farm." She extended her right arm with a graceful flourish. "How can you, in all good conscience, take a farm that beautiful, a farm that's been there for centuries, and slap a bunch of condos on it?"

"I'm not the one putting the condos up, remember? I'm just the guy making sure everybody understands the legalities and abides by them. Besides, the Bordens want to sell.

They're determined to sell. If they don't sell to Seatham, it'll be to someone else, that's guaranteed, and it might be to somebody with no aesthetic vision, no business ethics, no—"

"The Conservation Commission offered to buy it," she cut in crisply.

"Sure, for one-third the price. I know the Bordens are civic-minded people, but really, Marion..."

"Well, if you'd just give us some time to find funding..."

"There *is* no funding. Every budget in this town is strained to the limit." Geoff growled in frustration. "Marion, the development is going to be top-notch. What's your problem?"

"It's going to be an eyesore."

"It's going to be eminently tasteful."

"An eyesore," she insisted, crossing her arms tightly.

"Right. Not like that henhouse Hannah Borden hasn't used in two decades. You know, the one with the rat infestation? Now, that's really picturesque. We ought to make that a town landmark, bring school kids out here on field trips."

Marion's lips began to twitch. He hadn't meant to amuse her, dammit. He was angry.

"It's going to be a strain on the town's water supply," she argued, her control firmly back in place, "and on the school system and on snow removal crews..."

"Those aren't your problems," he said, enunciating each word carefully. "And the departments that do handle those problems don't seem too worried. Seatham has addressed all their concerns. If anything, the town is going to benefit. Think of the jobs in construction, in maintenance, in community services."

She slapped her forehead. "How could I forget?" she mocked. "We're going to become another Grosse Point from all the money that development's going to bring in."

Geoff wiped a hand over his mouth, pulling away the smile that was suddenly tickling at it. What the devil was the matter with him? This wasn't funny. "Let's face it, Marion," he said, scowling, "the only argument you have is based on opinion. On sentiment. You'd just rather keep the farm as it is."

"That's right. One of the goals of the Open Space Committee is to preserve the historical and rural character of this town. I don't take that responsibility lightly. And another thing—" she jabbed her index finger into his shirtfront "—that isn't our only argument. No one's addressed the sewage problem yet. Town pipes don't extend this far, and a septic system's going to leach right out to the marshes, and then—" she jabbed his chest again "—you and your Seatham pals are going to be in real deep—"

"Cow dung," he supplied.

She blinked. "What?"

"I find it really interesting that you're ready to take us to court over a sewage design we're still modifying—" his voice vibrated with conviction "—yet your committee never said boo about the high coliform count that developed in the marshes last year because of all the cow dung that washed down from the pastures above." He slapped his forehead, imitating her. "Oh, I forgot. Cows preserve the town's rural character. Dung is picturesque."

"Right," she asserted with a sparkle in her eyes. "About as picturesque as your left shoe right now."

Geoff glanced down and his face dropped. "My new Florsheim's!"

Marion pressed a hand hard across her mouth to stop a laugh, but it only seemed to spill from her eyes. He wanted to throttle her. Instead, he strode over to a patch of grass and wiped his shoe—sole, sides, toe—grumbling all the while.

Behind him he heard a muffled laugh. He turned to cast his wife an evil look, but suddenly he didn't want to do anything of the kind. Just wanted to stand there looking at her. At the sunlight gleaming through her silky hair. At the graceful curve of her smooth shapely legs as the breeze billowed her skirt....

"What?" She touched an uncertain hand to her hair, then to the base of her throat, as if he found something wrong or offensive in what he saw. He blinked. When had she become so touchy about her looks?

"Nothing," he said, frowning. "Nothing." He gazed out at the ocean. "I've got to head back into town. Got to be in court at one-thirty. A workman's comp case. Pretty routine."

"Mmm." She glanced at her watch. "I should be heading to the store, too."

They turned toward the footpath. "Sorry about interrupting your meditation," he said.

"That's okay. I don't think the gods had any answers for me today, anyway."

Geoff kept his eyes on the path as they descended toward their vehicles. She kept hers trained on the scrub growth. This interlude had been nice, he thought. A welcome break in the tension.

He reached his car and watched her climb into her truck. They were both heading into town, it was noon, and neither of them had eaten....

"Marion?" he called on impulse. She rolled down her window.

"Yes?"

This is absurd, he thought. *My heart is pounding as if I were a kid about to ask her for a date.*

His reaction sobered him. The reason his heart was pounding was that people who were three weeks away from separating didn't go out to lunch together.

"Uh...nothing. I'll be home—" he shrugged "—around ten."

CHAPTER FIVE

HE'D SAID TEN, but Geoff didn't come home until nearly one in the morning. Marion had stayed awake, unable to sleep, wondering where he was. No, not wondering. She knew where he was; that was the problem.

Now, staring at her puffy eyes in the bathroom mirror, she uttered a heartfelt, "Damn you, Geoffrey Kent!" Her stomach felt wretched, too, and she reached into the medicine cabinet for the antacid. The bottle, bought just last week, was nearly empty.

It was not a good way to start a Saturday, she thought, especially this Saturday. No matter how she felt, head splitting open or marriage falling apart, she had to work on Robyn's wedding. She especially needed to find a place to hold the reception. After booking the church, that was the most important detail to settle.

She showered quickly, dried her hair, then slipped into a comfortable cotton-knit dress, all the while aware of Geoff moving around in the kitchen below. As late as he'd come in, he'd still managed to get up before her. She was picking through her jewelry when she heard him leave for the office. He'd gotten into the habit of working Saturdays. She expelled a long breath, not sure if she was relieved he was gone—or disappointed.

The moment of confusion passed quickly. Of course she was relieved. Being with him was far too painful. No matter what mundane subject they might be discussing, she was forever haunted by the image of him with Tiffany, an image so painful she wondered how much longer she could endure it.

In the kitchen she pulled out the phone book from its drawer, along with a large notepad to jot down menus and prices. She figured she could do most of her preliminary work right here, calling around to see which places were available. Once she'd compiled a list, she'd drive out and check the sites in person.

Of course, she realized, all this running around could be avoided if she went through Weddings, Inc. Bronwyn would know immediately which restaurants and function rooms were available. She'd undoubtedly have a list far longer than the one the phone book could provide, too.

Marion considered calling her and apologizing, but she couldn't bring herself to do it. She couldn't take back her words. The legend *was* meaningless, the chapel *didn't* have any magic powers, and she was definitely in no mood to hear another of Bronwyn's lectures about how she and Geoff were made for each other. Besides, as she'd told Geoff yesterday, she'd manage.

Two hours later, though, Marion was sitting at the table with her head in her hands and despair in her heart. Planning a wedding in three weeks was insane! That was the moment she heard Geoff's car barrel into the driveway.

She sat up, back stiff, heartbeat accelerating. What was he doing home so early? The car door slammed and too soon he was climbing the back porch steps.

He walked in, tossed a newspaper and his briefcase on the table and went straight to the coffeepot. Marion glanced up to find him scowling.

"What?" she asked warily.

He returned to the table and set down his steaming mug. "Marion how could you do this?"

She sat straighter. "What?"

"This." He shoved the paper toward her, upsetting her notes.

She scanned the page. "Oh, it's my interview. I wasn't aware it would be in this week's edition." She grimaced at the photo taken of her in her studio. The girl who'd interviewed her was a college student working on the paper for the summer. Her talents with a camera left a lot to be desired.

The article was supposed to be a feature on Marion and her jewelry-making, but she'd managed to slide in her involvement with the Open Space Committee, too—as well as a few good zingers about Seatham. "Oh, for heaven's sake, Geoff, it's only a local interview. The town paper."

"I don't care. This paper reaches the right people, the voters." He paced, a hand pressed to the back of his neck. "When the hell did you become such an activist?"

Despite her exhaustion and defeated mood, she laughed. "A couple of measly quotes make me an activist?"

"Damn right they do!" He pulled out a chair, turned and straddled it, facing her.

"You look like hell, Geoffrey," she said.

"Good." He loosened his tie and unbuttoned the top button of his shirt. "That makes us matching bookends."

Marion stared at the scribbles on her notepad, feeling increasingly self-conscious. Unable to endure his scrutiny, she rose and went to the coffeemaker. But reaching for the pot, she changed her mind. Her stomach couldn't take another cup of coffee today.

She turned and saw him frowning at the bottle of antacid on the counter. "So, what is it about the article that's got you so riled?" she asked, leaning against the sink.

He pulled his gaze from the bottle, the hard lines returning to his face. "You fight dirty, Marion. All your punches are emotional. You tap into people's fears about the future of the planet. You even draw on their sense of patriotism. It's stupid—there isn't a single germane point to anything you say."

She crossed her arms tightly, her breath coming shorter and faster as the humiliation built. "Thank you very much. Now I'm stupid, on top of everything else."

Geoff paused, eyes narrowing. "On top of *what* everything else? What are you talking about?"

"Nothing." She looked aside. "Nothing."

Geoff took a sip of coffee, held the mug in two hands and stared into it, frowning. "It wasn't the proper forum, Marion. That was obviously supposed to be a profile of you as a jewelry designer."

"I'll take whatever forum I can get. Jeez, Geoff, you get to push Seatham's ideas on TV."

"Just the local cable station," he said defensively.

"Just? *Just?*" She made a strangled sound of frustration. "Do you realize how many people in this town watch that station? And that's above and beyond the exposure you get in the newspaper. You're in every issue. So don't lecture me about proper forum. I'll speak out whenever I can."

He pinned her with a sharp glance. "At the special town meeting?"

"If I have to," she replied, even though the thought hadn't entered her mind until that moment, and now that it had her stomach felt sicker than ever.

His scowl deepened, and watching him, Marion began to wonder if he was bothered by her opposition on a level she didn't quite grasp. It couldn't be insecurity. Geoff was the most confident capable person she knew.

Before she could gather her thoughts, however, the telephone rang. "Oh, that must be the Harborside. I called earlier to see about their function room." She picked up the receiver. "Hello?"

But it wasn't the restaurant. It was Lynn, the salesclerk who was working at the store. She was calling to ask if Marion could get someone else to come in for the afternoon. She wasn't feeling well.

While Geoff sat brooding over the newspaper, Marion made a call to another of her employees. Then another. No one could come. They'd all made plans that couldn't be changed. Sighing, Marion slumped forward until her forehead rested on the wall by the phone. Now what? She didn't want to go into the store herself, although she usually did work Saturdays. Today she had wedding errands to run.

When the phone rang right in her ear, she jumped a foot. Heart racing, she grappled with the receiver as if it were a slippery fish. "Yes?" This time, it *had* to be the restaurant.

But it wasn't. It was a friend in the artisans' co-op who was photographing some of her pieces for a new catalog. Feeling increasingly frazzled, Marion checked her calendar and set a date for the next shoot.

After saying goodbye, she called the store and told Lynn simply to close up for the day. With that done, she went to the refrigerator and poured herself a glass of milk to soothe her stomach. Geoff was staring at her, hawk-eyed, when she looked up. She wiped the mustache of milk from her upper lip and returned his look as boldly as she could. She was not overextended. She wasn't.

"Okay, um, what was it you were saying?" she asked.

He shook his head slowly. "I'll be damned if I can remember." The phone rang again.

Marion swirled the remaining milk in her glass, drank it down, then picked up the phone with false calm. "Yes?"

This time it was the call she'd been waiting for.

Unfortunately the manager of the Harborside couldn't oblige her with the answer she'd been waiting for. His function room was booked the day of Robyn's wedding.

After hanging up, Marion walked to the glass doors and stood staring out at the yard.

"Marion?"

She waved an arm behind her as if that might make Geoff disappear. "I can't talk about Seatham right now." The scratchiness of her voice dismayed her.

She heard him get up and walk over. The next moment his hands, warm and large and reassuring, were resting on her shoulders. She swallowed, or tried to, but the emotions he was arousing with his simple touch were just too overwhelming. Slowly, gently, his fingers began to knead the rock-hard muscles of her neck.

"What've you been doing all morning?" he asked, his breath feathering her hair. She shivered.

"Trying to find a place to have Robyn's reception."

"Not having any luck?"

Her vision blurred, but she blinked determinedly. "A couple of restaurants have rooms, but they're too small for our purposes. And then there's the Elks' hall. That's available. But, oh, Geoff..." She cast him a baleful look over her shoulder.

"Mm. Not exactly the Ritz, is it? How about the Haven Inn?"

"Booked."

"And the Wharf Tavern?"

"Even that."

He sighed, then offered philosophically, "You know, lots of people have had very nice receptions at the Elks' Hall. Couldn't the Van Bassens fill it with flowers or balloons or something?"

"We'd need a forest," she complained even though she was feeling somewhat better now that they were talking about the problem. "I suppose it wouldn't hurt to check the place out."

"Is there anything else that needs doing today?" His deep voice was having as soothing an effect on her nerves as his hands were. Her head lolled to one side.

"I was thinking of ordering the cake."

"Do you need help?" he asked.

"I'll manage."

He continued to stroke the tightness out of her shoulders. "Let me put it this way then—*let* me help."

"Why, for heaven's sake? You'd be bored silly."

He turned her around to face him, and she became consumed by the awareness that his hands remained on her upper arms. They were standing so close she could feel the heat radiating off his body, and for a moment, she felt woozy. "Well," he answered, "I was thinking that it might not be such a bad idea if we spent some time together today."

Her eyes darted to his. Almost simultaneously he released her and stepped away.

"What I mean is, it might be good for us to be seen together. You know, to quash any rumors that might be circulating about us." A frown creased his brow. "Last night Graham was telling me that some of his patients have been asking questions, questions as blatant as, are you and I still together."

"You were at Graham's last night?" She blinked owlishly.

He nodded and went on to detail a few other rumors he'd heard. But Marion wasn't listening. She was still stuck on the fact that he'd been at Graham's—when she'd been so certain he'd been with Tiffany.

"So, what do you say? Shall we go run your errands together?"

"Don't you have to go back to the office?"

"Uh-uh. I had a couple of clients call in and cancel their appointments and decided to have Freddie cancel the rest."

"I really can do this by myself."

"I know, but if you don't want your sister hearing gossip next time she's in town..."

Marion chewed on the inside of her cheek. She was disappointed that his offer didn't rise from a genuine desire to help her. Any kindness he extended would just be an act, a performance calculated to convince the world that they were still happily married. Still, for Robyn and Nate's sake, she'd be wise to go along with the idea.

"Okay. You have to be measured for a tux, anyway. Might as well be today."

"A tux?" He mimicked gagging. Nevertheless, he was already on his way down the hall. "Let me change into something more comfortable first. I won't be long."

It was a pleasant morning, warm, sunny, dry, and it would've been nice to believe that Geoff simply wanted to enjoy it with her when he suggested they walk into the town center. Nice but foolish. Marion didn't believe for a second he wanted to do anything but parade for the neighbors.

She didn't know why that bothered her so. She was in full agreement. She didn't need old Mrs. Hansen leaning over the fence when her parents were here for the wedding asking why she never saw Geoff and Marion together anymore.

Nevertheless, when Geoff reached for her hand on the front walk, she still jumped with surprise.

He looked at her askance, then a small teasing smile crooked his lips. "Is this a problem?" he asked, lifting her hand.

"No, of course not." She fixed her gaze ahead even while she was thinking, *Yes, it is a problem.* No matter how she tried to numb herself to it, the warmth, the strength in that hand—the familiarity of it—came through, and she didn't want to feel any of that anymore. It was time for that sort of thing to end.

They strolled the length of their tree-shaded lane, past front-yard gardens blooming with colorful perennials, past children running through lawn sprinklers.

Geoff wasn't drawn by their laughter as he had been at one time, and Marion was thankful he'd given that up. It used to pain her to see the longing in his eyes.

Water Street led directly to Bridge and their first destination, the Village Bakery.

"Do you know what to order?" Geoff asked, opening the bakery door.

"Uh-huh. I was on the phone for an hour last night with Robyn," she replied, stepping into the sweet-smelling shop. "I tried to persuade her to go with white or lemon, but you know Robyn. She insists on carrot cake with lots of raisins. At least I talked her out of chocolate. Do you have any idea what a nightmare chocolate cake is when you're trying to cover it with white frosting?"

Geoff smiled down at her, and her heart took an extra beat. Marion chided herself for being so vulnerable to him. That smile wasn't really meant for her but for Lucy, the woman watching them from behind the pastry-filled glass cases.

"Why, hello," Lucy exclaimed cheerily. "I haven't seen you two in quite some time." Her eyes returned to Geoff and she patted her tightly permed hair.

Marion suppressed a smile. Lucy was in her sixties but had never been able to hide the crush she had on Geoff.

"What can I get you? A few croissants for your breakfast tomorrow?"

Marion's hand tightened on the strap of her shoulder bag as images of Sundays past flashed through her mind. Croissants. Freshly ground coffee. The Sunday *Globe*. Geoff in his pajama bottoms, she in the top...

She chased the images away with an angry snap of her head. "No, Lucy. Today we need a wedding cake."

The woman's eyes sparkled. "Who's getting married? Not...Robyn?"

"Yes, Robyn."

Lucy clasped her hands and gasped incredulously, gazing at Geoff. "It seems only yesterday that child used to come in here with you."

He smiled softly. "My partner in crime. I used to use her as a excuse for coming in here so often."

"Oh, yes, you two did have a sweet tooth. So, when is this wedding, and what size cake will you need?"

It took a full half hour for all the details to be decided, but when the order was finally written up, Marion was pleased.

"Robyn's going to love it," she said, beaming, as they left the shop.

"Where to next?" Geoff asked, his hand drifting to the small of her back.

She tried to ignore the electrifying shivers racing over her. "Ted Webster's tux shop," she answered, reminding herself that whatever Geoff did was only for show, and she was being a first-class fool for reacting.

Ted Webster, whose mother owned the gown shop, seemed to be expecting them. "My mother told me the news. Robyn's biting the dust, eh?"

"Yes, and loving every minute of it." Marion smiled.

Ted clapped a hand on Geoff's shoulder. "And you're here to be fitted for a monkey suit, I take it."

Geoff grimaced. "Tell me something, Ted—why do we let women run weddings?"

"Hey, they keep me in business. Have a seat, Marion." And to Geoff he explained, "That's our director's chair."

Marion sat, while Ted efficiently went about the job of taking Geoff's measurements.

"Where's the reception going to be?" he asked, running a tape measure down Geoff's arm.

Marion's eyes followed the tape, mesmerized. "We're not sure yet. We're looking into our options today."

"Then I don't suppose you have a band yet, either."

"Uh-uh. Is your's available?"

Ted cast her an incredulous look. "Some of our bookings are made a year in advance." Ted played with a local band called the Honeymooners, its popularity due mostly to Kerry Muldoon, the talented young woman who was its leader and vocalist. "Well, I'm sure Bronwyn will come up with somebody good.

Marion merely nodded. "Ted, I have a question regarding tuxes. Nate has entrusted me with the job of choosing a style, but I don't know what he plans to do about getting fitted."

"No problem. Tell him to go into his nearest men's-wear shop to be measured and then call me with his measurements. How about the two fathers? Will they be wanting tuxes, too?"

"Yes, and there's an usher, Nate's brother-in-law. Should they do the same thing?"

"Yep. Happens all the time." Ted took a moment to jot down some figures. Then he dropped the pad and resumed measuring.

Marion sat back, enjoying the moment more than she cared to admit. Occasionally her eyes met Geoff's in the broad mirror. Once he rolled his eyes, and she knew this wasn't his favorite way to pass a Saturday. Another time he smiled and her mouth dried to cotton.

Ted whistled. "Still a thirty-two waist. How do you do it, man?" He slapped a hand to his own rather plump middle.

"Why don't you join the health club? Graham and I play racquetball there every Monday and Thursday night. That and the weight room—that's all I usually do. But there's a running track and a pool..."

Geoff went on listing the club's many features, but Marion, for the second time that day, was too dumbstruck to hear. Racquetball. How could she have forgotten? That's where he'd been Thursday night.

"Okay, Marion." Ted looped the yellow tape around his neck. "Formal? Casual? What sort of event are we talking here?"

"I'd say...semiformal. Daytime."

"Traditional?"

"Please." She shuddered, glancing toward a wall of pastels.

Ted went to the blacks and grays and started pulling suits. "Okay, Counselor. Let's put on a fashion show for the lady."

Minutes later Geoff returned from the dressing room to model the first tux. Sitting in her director's chair, Marion tilted her head to one side, then to the other, trying to pretend her heart hadn't stopped. She'd forgotten how magnificent Geoff looked in a tux. His wide shoulders and strong chest filled out the coat wonderfully, while the white pleated shirt emphasized the coppery cast of his tanned skin. Her eyes traveled the length of him. "That boy has the longest legs I've ever seen," she remembered her mother commenting when they'd first started dating. Now Marion smiled unthinkingly, admiring how elegant those long legs made the outfit look.

"I like it," she said noncommittally, "but let's see the others before we decide."

The second suit was similar to the first, except that it included a waistcoat and a striped four-in-hand that Geoff had tied too hastily. Marion rose from her seat.

"Wait a sec," she said softly, adjusting the knot. Inadvertently her knuckles brushed the warm rough skin of his neck and a flame licked over her. Her fingers fumbled. "Sorry," she whispered, while he stood very still, his dark penetrating eyes fixed on her flushed face.

Pinned under his gaze, she experienced a shortness of breath she knew he could detect. "There." She smoothed a hand down the tie, feeling the heat and hardness of his chest through the layers of fabric. She bit her lip, not daring to look up.

It wasn't right that this should be happening—this dizzy excitement, this electrified awareness. Not after what he'd done. Not when they were planning to separate. What was the matter with her? Had she no pride?

On legs of rubber, she stepped away.

He tried on the rest of the suits, but they finally decided on the first. Geoff retreated to the dressing room to change back into his faded jeans and navy polo shirt. Marion followed him with her eyes.

With a start she realized that Ted was watching her. He laughed when she blushed.

"Hey, no need to be embarrassed. I only hope Ruthie is still looking at me that way when we've been married as long as you two have. How long is it, anyway?"

"It'll be eleven years next month. How much do I owe you?" she said quickly, hoping to distract him.

They were just squaring away the deposit when Geoff returned.

"Marion tells me your anniversary is coming up soon," Ted said while he wrote out a receipt. "Planning anything special?"

Neither of them moved.

"Not sure yet," Geoff said vaguely. He glanced at his watch. "Well, we've got to run. Lots more errands. Don't forget—the health club. Stop by some time."

Outside again, they hurried across the old stone bridge that spanned the Sussex River and turned onto First Street. Neither of them said a word or looked at each other.

He doesn't want to be reminded of another anniversary any more than I do, Marion thought, crossing the street.

Their next destination was the Elks' Hall, beyond the green, just past the Old Burial Ground.

An hour later they were retracing their steps, their clothing sticking to their backs. Marion's feet were dragging.

In the middle of Soldier's Green, Geoff paused to get a drink from a granite water fountain. Straightening, he wet his hands and pressed them to Marion's flushed face. She closed her eyes, sighing under his cool touch.

"Have you come to a decision about the hall?" he asked.

"Yes. I don't like it. It's worse than I remembered." She stepped up to the fountain and took a drink. "I don't know what to do, Geoff."

He squinted out over the green, over the flower beds and towering trees, toward the library and the Town Hall, to the county courthouse where he spent so much of his time. "I do," he finally said. "Let's go have lunch."

Marion couldn't help laughing. "That's the best idea yet."

The Bridge Street Café had existed as long as Marion could remember, although recently it had added an outdoor patio overhanging the river. She and Geoff were seated at one of the new umbrella-covered tables right by the rail.

The back side of the cedar-shingled restaurant displayed an engaging array of lobster-trap buoys, oars, bells and fish netting, while wooden tubs of petunias, scattered randomly across the deck, added bright summer color.

"What are you going to order?" Marion asked, skimming the menu.

"Fried clams. What else?" Fried clams were the house specialty.

"That does sound good. Make that a double." Marion closed her menu. She felt strange sitting here with her husband. They hadn't been out to eat in... well, she couldn't remember the last time. Stranger still, her nerves were buzzing sort of the way they used to when she and Geoff were dating.

"I have an idea regarding Robyn's wedding," he offered hesitantly. "I'm not sure you'll like it, but..."

"I'll like anything right about now. What is it?"

"Well, how about having the reception at our house?"

His suggestion took her so by surprise she opened her mouth but nothing came out.

"You know, a garden party."

"Are you sure you know what you're letting yourself in for? People overrunning the place, guests, caterers, musicians..."

He shrugged carelessly.

"And the weather. Garden parties are at the absolute mercy of the weather, and here in New England you're just begging for disaster."

"That's why tent rentals are such big business."

Her mind whirled. "It's going to be a lot of work, Geoff. Making arrangements. Getting the yard ready..."

"We have three weeks."

She stared at his impossibly handsome face, into his dark fathomless eyes, trying to gauge the sincerity in that word "we." Unexpectedly and quite irrationally, she experienced a feeling of connectedness with him, with his confidence and strength, and with it came a feeling that all things were possible.

"Oh, Geoff." She covered her mouth with the fingertips of two hands. "It would be lovely, wouldn't it?"

He nodded. "Let's do it, Marion. You want Robyn to have a beautiful wedding...."

She laughed, unable to contain her bubbling joy. "Okay. All right. Let's do it."

He smiled, his gaze roaming her face. "Feel better?"

"Immensely. As soon as I get home I'll call Carl Hubbard for a tent."

"Does he provide tables and chairs, too?"

"I'm sure he must. And the Silvas' catering service has tablecloths and china and silverware." She paused. "That's assuming we'll be able to get the Silvas to cater for us."

"Come on, Marion. After all the pro bono work I've done for them?"

Marion took in a deep clear breath. It felt like the first easy breath in a week.

Their food arrived and they dug in, chatting animatedly about the wedding. When Marion had finished her meal, she could hardly believe how fast time had flown.

What a lovely day this has been, she thought, reclining against the deck rail and gazing bemusedly at the river sliding below them. *Why haven't we done this more often? It would've been so easy, too, working as we do right across the street from each other. Why did we wait until now, when we're about to break up?*

"A penny for your thoughts," Geoff murmured.

Marion sat up, smiling shyly. "I was just remembering how we used to have lunch together all the time when we were first married."

Geoff picked up his mug of beer, drained the dregs and squinted off at a point across the river. Marion wondered what *he* was remembering. The attic apartment they used to rent not far from here? How, every day, they'd walked to work together hand in hand?

Mornings used to tick by so slowly those days, until at noon they'd dash from their respective doors, meeting with an impassioned kiss, not caring who saw....

When the weather permitted, they'd take their brown-bagged lunch to the green and have a picnic. At other times they'd splurge and eat here or at the diner. And sometimes...sometimes they'd simply return to their attic rooms and skip lunch entirely.

Marion peeked at her husband—he was looking back—and a coil of heat tightened deep inside her. Wetting her parched lips with the tip of her tongue, she glanced aside.

This crazy reaction didn't mean anything, she told herself. It was the *memory* of their lovemaking that was making her so dizzy.

But a second look confirmed what she already knew but didn't care to admit. Despite every bad thing that had ever come between them, Geoff still had the power to stir her physically. Even now. Even here.

Suddenly she noticed his right eyebrow lift, his stare become surprised, perhaps a little amused. He'd once told her he could always tell when she had sex on her mind. Now Marion didn't know where to settle her gaze.

"We'd b-better be heading to the house," she stammered. "Lots of phone calls to make."

He agreed. "I just want to make a stop in the men's room before we go." He rose. "Be back in a minute."

It wasn't until he was gone that Marion noticed they hadn't been alone. Across the deck, watching her like an assassin, sat Tiffany Taylor.

CHAPTER SIX

TIFFANY UNCOILED from her seat and walked across the patio, leaving a well-dressed gentleman sitting by himself at her table. "Hello, Mrs. Kent."

Marion wondered if her hearing was faulty or if Tiffany really had invested the "Mrs." part of her greeting with sarcasm. Was she rubbing in the fact that she knew the title was only temporary?

Marion couldn't bring herself to say hello back. "Did you want to speak with Geoff? He's just gone inside for a minute." Her gaze slid over the young woman's attire. Although it was a Saturday, Tiffany was dressed in a smart ivory suit with an emerald silk blouse, high-heeled shoes and exquisite gold jewelry. The blouse, Marion noticed, matched Tiffany's eyes exactly. Today her long black hair was arranged in a soft feminine topknot.

"No, actually. I want to speak with you." Tiffany sat in Geoff's chair uninvited.

"Me?"

"That's right. I want you to know how awful I feel about what happened to you last week. You know, walking into Geoff's office when you did? I'm so very sorry that happened." Her voice was earnest, her eyes sympathetic, but instinct told Marion to be cautious.

"I'm aware that you and Geoff have been having problems in your marriage..."

A knife seemed to lodge in Marion's midsection. Geoff had talked to this woman, this stranger, about their problems? And which problems?

"But I never meant to be the catalyst that would split you two up. Naturally I think he's an attractive man. Who doesn't? But I do have my principles, Mrs. Kent."

Marion's head began to throb, she was thinking so hard, trying to figure out what Tiffany was really saying. Was she implying her principles allowed her to go around kissing married men as long as she didn't wreck their marriages? Or was she saying they had been doomed to split anyway, whether she interfered or not? One thing that jumped out clearly enough, though, was that she knew Geoff had moved out last week.

"You haven't split us up. Geoff's moved back," Marion responded out of hurt pride before she had time to think. Within three weeks Tiffany would know this arrangement was all a sham.

Tiffany's expression dropped almost imperceptibly, a slightly startled look entering her eyes. But then she smiled. "Good. Good. I'm so glad." She even reached across the table and squeezed Marion's arm. "I think the world of your husband, you know. He's one of the brightest, most charming people I've ever worked with."

Marion became a little confused by Tiffany's overt admiration. Surely someone with designs on another woman's husband wouldn't be so open with her praise.

"He's the most compatible partner I've ever had, too," Tiffany added. "We work extremely well together, and I'd like to continue working with him in the future—with your blessing, of course. Our relationship is purely professional. I want you to understand that, especially now that we've both been offered this wonderful opportunity on the West Coast." She paused just a heartbeat to study Marion's face. "I wouldn't want any personal misunderstandings between you and me to influence his decision."

As Tiffany's words sank in, a trembling started in the pit of Marion's stomach and spread through her entire frame.

Tiffany moved in closer, smiling as if they were lifelong friends. "I don't suppose you could give me a clue which way he's leaning...."

"Uh . . . no." That was all Marion could get out past her confusion and pain.

"I do hope he accepts the job. He'd be a wonderful asset to Seatham and, well, you must know how tired he is of small-town cases. A man with just half Geoff's abilities would suffocate here." She shuddered ever so delicately. "Coming to work for Seatham, he'll be traveling, meeting exciting people. It'll do wonders for his outlook, to say nothing about how well off he'll be financially. Sorry—how well off *you'll* be. That is, if Seatham lets you tag along," she teased with a light friendly laugh. "Believe me, your opposition to our project hasn't gone unnoticed." But then Tiffany's smile faded and she added with concern, "It hasn't done Geoff any good, either."

Marion was so numb she didn't even realize Geoff had returned until Tiffany rose and greeted him. Marion seemed to have dropped into a fog, voices around her muffled, actions distorted.

The man sitting at Tiffany's table came over and Geoff introduced him. Marion didn't catch the name. Someone with Seatham. Numb, she didn't follow their banter, either, missed the point of their jokes.

What she didn't miss, however, were the deep meaningful glances Tiffany kept giving her husband and the way she leaned toward him when she talked, so that her breast brushed his arm. Then, just before parting, she made a point of reminding Geoff of an appointment they had on Monday, naming people and affairs that Marion knew nothing about.

Geoff and Marion walked home in near silence. He asked if she was okay. She said yes, a very clipped yes. He asked if seeing Tiffany had upset her, and she said no. Good, he said, because there was nothing to be upset about, and then he dropped the subject, allowing her to sink deeper into her thoughts.

When Marion had told Bronwyn she and Geoff had drifted apart, she hadn't really known how far. He'd been offered a job with Seatham, on the West Coast, no less, and hadn't breathed a word to her about it. Yet Tiffany knew. Tiffany knew lots of things about Geoff that Marion didn't. Important things. Like he was bored with his small-town practice. That he longed for the excitement of working with a large firm. She knew how much money he was going to make, knew Marion's affiliation with the Open Space Committee was giving him problems, knew their marriage had been in trouble for some time...

The more Marion thought about it, the more alienated from Geoff she felt.

No wonder he hadn't told her about the job offer. Whether or not he went to work for Seatham had nothing to do with her. Her opinion didn't count. That scenario was part of his future... Life after Marion... Three thousand miles away... With Tiffany... Tiffany was being transferred, too.

As that last fact took root, Marion became convinced that her suspicions regarding Geoff and Tiffany had been accurate. She'd have to be a fool to believe it was mere coincidence that both Tiffany and Geoff had been offered jobs at the same office so far away. It had happened because somebody had pulled a few strings. And why? Why else? They wanted to be together.

What cut deepest, though, was the realization that Tiffany was such a good match for Geoff. She shared the same profession; she was bright and outgoing, and they worked well together. Tiffany had said it best: he was the most compatible partner she'd ever had.

Most likely, she was also able to have children. Marion couldn't ever forget that.

Geoff opened the front gate in their white picket fence, and as Marion went up the walk ahead of him, she was reminded of that snow-dusted evening seven years ago when he'd brought her here to celebrate their being approved for a mortgage. How different their future had seemed then. How many disappointments they'd suffered since.

Now Geoff was being offered another chance. Work that would challenge and stimulate him. A salary that finally matched his abilities. A vibrant woman who would be the sort of helpmate he deserved. And the possibility of a family.

Marion finally understood why he hadn't had any qualms about moving back here with her until the wedding. No danger of *him* indulging in occassional flights of sentimentality. No danger of *him* feeling any sexual discomfort. He'd known all along he would be leaving, and he'd known his destination. It had been a certainty.

Well, maybe it was time she faced the music, too, and finally admitted, really admitted, their marriage was over.

GEOFF UNLOCKED the front door and watched Marion march down the hall to the kitchen. He followed in her tense wake, wondering what the *hell* had gotten into her now. For a while today she'd almost been her old self. She'd looked relaxed as they'd walked around town, happy as they'd eaten lunch. And he—he had begun to feel he had a function in her life once more.

But she'd pulled into herself again, the coolness and distance back in place, effectively sealing him out.

As he leaned in through the kitchen doorway watching her, she opened the phone book and looked up the number of Carl Hubbard's tent-rental place.

"Don't you have anything to do?" she inquired frostily.

He raised his hands. "I'm going, I'm going." And without further argument he grabbed his briefcase, and the newspaper and retreated to his study. Obviously meeting Tiffany *had* upset her—which was a mystery to him. Tiffany had never exhibited anything but the most professional behavior, except for that one night when she'd kissed him, and even that had been too clearly innocent to affect Marion the way it had.

Geoff sat at his desk and leaned on his elbows, sinking his fingers into his hair. Marion's behavior didn't make sense—except when he looked at it in one particular light: she'd latched onto poor Tiffany as an excuse, blowing the incident all out of proportion merely to have a reason to get out of their marriage.

The newspaper lay in front of him, still open to Marion's interview. Now his eyes focused on the photograph of her modeling a pair of her earrings, each a cascading cluster of small bronze and copper leaves. In the background hung her preliminary sketches for the design. In spite of his foul mood, he smiled, a stream of pride flowing through him.

He turned his attention to the interview, this time ignoring her gibes against Seatham. She'd told the reporter how she'd gotten started—how her father had noticed her fascination with popping together toy beads when she was a toddler and how he'd come home from a flea market with a half-bushel basket full of junk jewelry for her, to replace the toy beads....

Geoff rested his chin on his palm and stared into space. When he'd met her, she'd been only nineteen, but she'd had a serenity about her that had just about blown him away. She'd known who she was, where she was going—and apparently she'd known all her life.

Her inner calm was a quality that had always drawn him to her and yet saddened him. He didn't feel a part of it, part of the core that kept her centered. It had been there before him and would be there long after he left.

He heard the phone on his desk faintly click and knew by the sound she'd just hung up—for the third time. It appeared renting a tent on three weeks' notice wasn't as easy as they'd thought.

He returned to the article, to the question about where she got ideas for her designs. Geoff's vision turned inward again, to a memory of coming down to breakfast one morning and finding her with her nose to a magnifying glass, studying a moth asleep on a window screen—a big brown thing that he at first thought was a dead leaf. "Come here," she'd called. "Isn't he amazing!" And for a long timeless while he'd joined her in her inspection.

Geoff abruptly got up from his desk, went to the bar and poured himself a glass of something strong. Marion saw beauty in things no one else noticed, and for a few precious years she'd opened that world to him. He didn't think she understood how much he appreciated that. In a career where he rubbed shoulders with scum almost daily, he needed to come home to her vision. He needed to be reassured there was beauty and goodness in the world.

He downed the smooth bourbon and immediately poured another shot. He didn't like their being on opposite sides of a public issue. Not because he got flack from Seatham higher-ups. Not even because it was a little embarrassing to be openly challenged by his own wife. No, the reason ran deeper than that. While he wasn't about to nominate Marion for sainthood, she'd always represented a kind of goodness to him, and without her by his side, he felt... He didn't want to say uncertain, but something sure as hell wasn't right.

Rationally, it made no sense. There was nothing wrong with his representing Seatham. He'd investigated the firm carefully, examined their plans and found nothing at odds with his personal or professional code of ethics.

Yet, having drifted from Marion, he felt, well, as if he'd lost his grounding. Like those astronauts floating in space he remembered watching on TV when he was a kid.

Strange—for a while this afternoon, he'd felt a connection with her again. Maybe he should suggest they do something tonight. Rent a movie. Order in a pizza. See if he could rediscover that link.

He left his study and returned to the kitchen, but Marion wasn't there. Then he heard a movement from her studio.

He walked to the door. She was sitting with her back to him, engrossed in her work. In the golden light of the lowering sun she looked beautiful, soft, touchable. And suddenly Geoff wanted to touch her and knew the need had been building all day.

"Marion?" he called, but she didn't turn. It was then that he realized she was wearing earphones. She was listening to music, totally oblivious to him.

For several minutes Geoff stood there watching her, unnoticed, feeling increasingly alone.

No, there would be no movie tonight. No shared pizza. He knew from experience she'd be in here for hours, perfectly content, not needing anything to sustain her but the flow of her work. Certainly she didn't need him.

Geoff went back to his study, called O'Toole at his Boston hotel and asked when he could fly out to California. The less time he spent in this house the better.

"If you can clear your schedule," O'Toole said, "we can have you in the air by Thursday afternoon. How's that?"

"Sounds good. I'm looking forward to it."

Geoff hung up and thought of pouring himself another drink. Instead, he drove to the health club and worked out on the weight machines until every muscle in his body was screaming. Saturday night alone at a health club, he thought, sitting exhausted in the whirlpool afterward. Life wasn't supposed to be this way.

ON MONDAY MORNING Geoff asked Freddie to rearrange his calendar so he'd be free for the junket to Carmel. Freddie, a friend of Robyn's who'd been with Geoff since her graduation from secretarial school four years ago, peered at him. "That'll mean working late, Mr. K. Real late."

"I know." He watched Freddie's mouth tighten.

"Is, um, that Ms. Taylor going to California, too?"

"No, Freddie. That Ms. Taylor's staying in Boston."

She nodded—as if it was her business to approve or disapprove of his company. Then, "Is this trip really necessary?"

"Yes," he said, growing irritated. He poured himself a cup of coffee, hurried up the stairs to his private office and shut the door.

Picking up the phone, he punched in Graham's home number. Because his friend was half out the door on his way to his own office, Geoff wasted no time in explaining he couldn't meet for racquetball that week.

"You're going where?" Graham blasted over the receiver. "Oh, man, you're blowing it. Two and a half measly weeks left to save your marriage and you're taking off?"

"There's nothing to save. How many times do I have to tell you that?"

"Is that Tiffany going?"

"No!" What was this thing people had about Tiffany?

He hung up, feeling a headache coming on. By the time he got home, it was a major thumper. But he hadn't told Marion about the trip yet and didn't think it was wise to put something that important off till the last minute.

She was working in her studio, and when he told her, her shoulders flinched. Still, her eyes remained fixed on her soldering. In fact, since coming home from lunch on Saturday, she'd barely looked at him at all.

"What's this trip about?" She sounded perfectly calm, though he'd never seen the lines around her mouth quite so hard.

"Nothing too important. Seatham's trying to buy a parcel of land and needs me to help their legal team get started on studying local building codes and zoning restrictions, that sort of thing."

"I see." A pulse was beating at her temple. "How long will you be gone?"

"I'll be leaving Thursday afternoon and returning next Tuesday. Is that okay with you?"

She shrugged. "Doesn't matter. Do what's best for you." And she'd gone on with her work.

Geoff retreated to his study, kicking himself for having asked. He'd been hoping she'd be upset, or at least more curious. How many times did he have to set himself up to be shot down before he realized Marion didn't give a damn where he went. When would he ever learn?

BY THURSDAY AFTERNOON Marion could avoid the fact no longer. The situation with Geoff was having a seriously detrimental effect on her health. Ever since the argument that had precipitated his moving out, her stomach had been so nervous she'd vomited almost every day. Her appetite was nonexistent and her sleep patterns so disturbed she was afraid that one day she was simply going to drop from exhaustion.

She supposed the situation was understandable. To have the foundation of your life kicked out from under you was no laughing matter, and being Geoff's wife *had* been her foundation. She knew that wasn't a popular attitude for a woman to espouse these days, but somehow Marion had always felt enlarged by defining herself as Geoff's wife, not diminished. She couldn't explain it; it was just something she'd felt.

Apparently she'd been a fool. Now, facing life alone, she realized she should have examined her attitude more carefully and recognized the dangers inherent in it. No woman was secure. Commitment was merely a word, a puff of breath with no substance.

That afternoon she called her doctor and was able to slide in an appointment the next morning. Technically Dr. Toomey was an ob-gyn specialist, but Marion's gynecological history was so complex and the hours she'd spent in his office so numerous that she'd come to view him as her primary-care physician, as well.

"What's up, Marion?" He was a thin stoop-shouldered man with merry eyes and a kind smile.

Marion relayed her physical ailments, careful to avoid mentioning Geoff as a cause. "I've just taken on too much. Too many irons in the fire. And now with Robyn's wedding..." She merely shrugged, hoping her speechlessness would convey the extent of her stress. "I wondered if you could give me something to relax, a mild tranquilizer, maybe, just until my life calms down a little."

The white-haired physician nodded sagely. "Of course, of course. But first I'd like to run a few tests. Nothing to get alarmed about, but I want to be sure what we're dealing with. Who knows, you could be carrying some exotic virus that'll make me famous."

Marion saw no point to his tests. She was sure she had a simple case of nerves brought on by the circumstances of her life, and once those circumstances were resolved, she'd be back to normal. Still, she understood his caution.

She didn't expect to get results that very afternoon. She'd been told that some of the lab work would take a couple of days. And she certainly didn't expect to hear what Dr. Toomey had to say. In fact, it was the very last thing on her mind.

"I'm *what?*" she squeaked into the phone in the back room of her store.

"Congratulations, Marion. You're pregnant."

CHAPTER SEVEN

MARION MARCHED into Dr. Toomey's office and straight to his desk, ignoring the chair he was gesturing her toward.

"There must be a mistake." She leaned over the desk, resting her weight on her fingertips.

He threw back his head and laughed. "No mistake about it, Marion. I'd say you're about six weeks along. Have a seat."

She remained standing. "But it's impossible!"

"Marion, it was never impossible. Just difficult."

Marion stared at the stethoscope hooked around his neck, seeing nothing, hearing nothing. A roaring in her ears drowned out everything in the present. From what seemed a long distance away she heard herself ask, "Are you sure?"

And he answered, "Quite."

Without knowing how she got there, she found herself sitting in the chair, gripping the upholstered arms as if she were on a faster-than-light rocket ride.

"We can run the test again if you'd like, but..."

"Yes, let's. And I'll wait for the results, if you don't mind."

He shrugged. "If it'll make you feel better." He paged his nurse who escorted Marion to one of the examining rooms.

A few minutes later she was back in his office feeling supremely self-righteous. *He'd* see.

"The upset stomach you've complained about might very well be the result of stress," he admitted, "but it could also be a case of morning sickness. My guess is it's a combination of both." As he spoke his pen scratched across a small pad. "I'm going to give you a prescription. It should help, but it isn't a tranquilizer. Instead, *you're* going to be your own best medicine. I want you to make a conscious effort to relax. A couple of times a day, take a break, walk, listen to soothing tapes—whatever you find most effective. At the same time, cut down on whatever's getting you wired—caffeine, work hours."

Marion continued to stare at him, stunned speechless. Had he gone mad? Why was he perpetuating this folly about a pregnancy?

He laughed softly. "Honestly, if you could only see your face. I'm sorry, I shouldn't find this so amusing. Knowing what you've gone through to get to this day, I should've broken the news differently." His smile faded. "Perhaps I should've called Geoff in here, too."

"No!" Although she didn't have a single coherent idea at the moment, she knew instinctively she didn't want Geoff to be a part of this. "Don't apologize. I...I'm fine." Her pulse pounded.

The physician's eyes turned concerned. "Marion, I know you went through the wringer a few years ago, and I can see you're worried now, but we corrected the problem that caused your miscarriages. There's no reason to believe you won't carry this baby to full term."

This baby? His words still weren't making sense. She hadn't simply had a problem with endometriosis; she was practically infertile. When Marion Kent screwed up, she did it thoroughly.

Just then the nurse returned, placed a folder in front of the doctor and smiled at Marion before leaving. Marion moved to the edge of her seat, perspiration trickling down her sides.

The doctor opened the folder, nodded, then turned it for her to see. Sure enough, right under the tip of his index finger was the word "positive."

Marion reeled. It couldn't be, not when she and Geoff were about to go their separate ways. Why not a few years ago when they'd been so desperate to have a child they would've walked through fire for one?

"I don't understand." Her voice was barely audible, all the strength having drained out of her. "We tried so hard. We had the world's best experts working with us in Boston, the most advanced technology..."

"Sometimes it just happens this way, and it's not for us to understand."

"But I'd given up. So had Geoff."

Dr. Toomey looked at her with deepening concern. "Is this pregnancy going to cause a problem?"

She felt her cheeks warming. "No, no, of course not."

"You seem upset."

"Well, it's just..." Just what? That her husband was now in California, eagerly exploring the area where his future lay and a baby was the very last thing he needed? "We went through all the trouble of adjusting our life-style and way of thinking," she temporized, "and now we have to adjust everything back."

Dr. Toomey smiled sympathetically. "Just keep in mind how young you are. Thirty-one, is it?"

She nodded.

"That would make Geoff thirty-three. Babies yourselves. Far too young to be set in your ways or to think you won't be able to cope with a child. Why, I had a woman in here only last week, forty-three and pregnant for the first time. She was so thrilled she was bouncing like a jumping bean."

Marion obliged him with a smile, but really she didn't want to hear about other women. She reached for her prescription.

"Not so fast. I have another to write out. Vitamins," he explained, scribbling. Then he swiveled his chair and pulled a pamphlet off a shelf. "Everything you'll need to know is in here—diet, exercise, physical changes each trimester."

"Thank you." Marion took the prescriptions and information without meeting his eyes. They'd been through all this before, twice. She knew what to expect. Suddenly a dark empty space opened up inside her.

"I have a favor to ask," she said, trying hard to conceal her sadness. "If you happen to run into Geoff, will you please not mention that I'm pregnant?"

The physician's white eyebrows met over puzzled eyes.

"He's off on a business trip until next Tuesday, but when he does return, please... He's extremely busy with this Seatham development right now." She glanced away. "He has other concerns, too, an important career decision to make, a tough trial coming up." She told herself she wasn't really lying. Not a month went by that Geoff didn't have a fairly sticky court case to deal with. "He's awfully taxed right now and doesn't need anything else to worry about. I prefer to wait and tell him later."

The doctor tilted his head. "I can't see what he'd have to be worried about. The news might even give him a lift."

"No," she replied adamantly. "I know Geoff. It would only distract him, and right now he doesn't need any more distractions."

The doctor raised a staying hand. "Okay, no problem. You tell him when you feel the time is right."

"Thank you." She breathed a sigh of relief.

The doctor rose. "Oh, on your way out remind my receptionist to write up a schedule of appointments for you. I'll need to see you regularly."

"Certainly."

Marion left the office in a daze, afraid that her legs wouldn't get her even to her truck. She turned the key in the ignition and pulled away from the curb without knowing where she was going.

She drove aimlessly for at least half an hour, yet a certain homing instinct must have quietly kicked in, because, without consciously knowing how she got there, she found herself parked in front of the Powell estate. The lump in her throat was as big as a fist. She needed to talk to someone, needed to share her news and lift some of this weight off her shoulders.

But how could she knock on Bronwyn's door after the way they'd argued last week? Besides, what did she expect to get out of sharing her news? Sympathy? Courage? Bronwyn would give neither. She'd undoubtedly go off into raptures about how the pregnancy was a sign Marion and Geoff were meant to stay together.

Marion put her truck in motion again. She considered stopping by the co-op store, maybe talking to the friends she had there, but that thought didn't even make it off the runway. They wouldn't understand these feelings choking her. Bronwyn might, but not her artist friends. They knew only a limited aspect of her life, the aspect involved with jewelry-making and jewelry-marketing, and that, she realized, was a limited aspect indeed.

As so often happened when she was troubled, Marion drove out to the beach and hiked up Mattasquamicutt Hill. There, sitting on her favorite rock, she gazed out over the ocean and let her thoughts drift. Now, it all made sense—her sleeplessness, her nausea and, of course, her recent bouts with the weepies.

While she sat there, staring at the glittering water, her tensions gradually eased and the knowledge peacefully entered her heart: she was pregnant.

With the realization just now sinking in, she placed her hands over her abdomen and her eyes filled with tears. She was pregnant. She was carrying a new life.

Awestruck and giddy, she alternately cried and laughed, and was deeply relieved no one else was on the hill to see her foolishness.

Moving a hand lightly across her stomach, she wondered if telling Geoff might not give their marriage a new lease on life. But she shook the idea off within seconds. That was a terrible burden to lay on a child. If she, without a child, wasn't enough to hold Geoff's interest, then with a child, she shouldn't be enough, either, and she certainly didn't want him staying around out of a sense of obligation.

Especially now that he had this wonderful opportunity opening up with Seatham on the West Coast. Lord, he was already out there working on their next project, that's how eager he was to get started. He'd tried to tell her the job was temporary—a deception that still offended her—but she wouldn't be surprised if he was already checking out apartments. If he stayed here, he would only turn resentful toward her, and maybe even toward the child.

In fact, if she really wanted everyone's best interest to be served, as soon as he got home Tuesday she'd initiate a discussion about divorce proceedings—when to begin, how. It was a subject they'd both been avoiding, and the mere thought sickened her, but with the subject out in the open he'd probably feel less guilty about the opportunities awaiting him. If she could keep up a dispassionate front, pretending she really didn't mind the prospect of being divorced, he'd undoubtedly feel freer to make his decisions.

She rested her chin on her knees, staring ahead into forever. If she was truly honest, though, there was one other reason she wanted to keep the news of her pregnancy from Geoff. She'd been pregnant before but had miscarried, and she hadn't a single real doubt she'd lose this baby, too, no matter what Dr. Toomey said. The question wasn't *if* she'd lose it but *when,* and she saw no reason to get Geoff needlessly involved. He'd suffered so much the other times, it would actually be kinder not to involve him, not to lift his hopes only to destroy them within a few weeks. He'd had enough of that, enough to last a lifetime.

No, her first instincts were right. She'd keep her news to herself and face whatever happened alone.

Her hand drifted to her abdomen again. Under her palm beat the heart of a new life. She couldn't actually feel the beat, but she knew it was there. She sensed it in her very cells.

How long will I have you, little one? she wondered. *How long this bittersweet joy?* Her question lifted on the wings of the wind, but Marion didn't wait for a response. This was one question she didn't want to have answered.

Feeling more at peace, she climbed down the hill, but instead of going directly home, she detoured to a neighboring town where no one knew her and had her prescriptions filled. At home she tucked everything in her underwear drawer—vitamins, medication, appointment cards and brochures—and turned her thoughts to dinner.

Early evening cast bars of light and shadow across the backyard and into her kitchen. Like living underwater, she thought, as she pulled a microwave dinner from the freezer. And like underwater, silence filled the house, amplifying the ticking of the banjo clock in the next room.

She popped the meal into the microwave and pressed the appropriate buttons, trying to ignore her expanding sense of loneliness.

While the food warmed, she flicked on the small TV on the counter and then picked up the phone, and as the microwave hummed and the TV quietly babbled, she spoke to her mother in Florida, filling her in on all the latest wedding news. Throughout the conversation she suffered the urge to talk about her pregnancy, but when she cradled the receiver a few minutes later, she was still as bottled up as ever.

Taking the hot plastic dish out of the microwave, she perched on a stool in front of the television and peeled back the cellophane. By now the evening light had been completely overtaken by shadow. She sat in the gloom, telling herself she didn't feel alone. She didn't feel frightened. This was how she'd spent innumerable nights in the recent past, and she was used to it.

But the feeling of dread continued to grow. This loneliness wasn't the same. It was deeper, sharper, had something to do with the new life inside her.

Suddenly the newscast flickering on the small screen drew her attention. "Turning now to the ongoing controversy involving the Seatham Corporation..."

Marion's eyes opened wide just as the screen broke away from the newscaster and filled with an image of Geoff, Geoff sitting on some cypress-shaded patio overlooking the Pacific, his thick dark hair tossing across his forehead in a stiff breeze.

Marion slowly lowered her fork and with great difficulty swallowed her food. She was watching the local cable station, so it wasn't unusual to see Geoff on the screen. Nobody in the community was safe from WETE programmers. What was unusual, however, was seeing him broadcast from the opposite coast. In all likelihood it was a tape.

The news Geoff relayed in his calm confident manner should have made her angry. Seatham had just that day offered Eternity a quarter of a million dollars to be put into the school-department budget—pending, of course, the approval of their building plans. The gift was meant to allay current fears that taxes would rise because of the dozens of new children pouring into the Eternity school system from the Seatham development, which was now being called Saltmarsh Farm.

"Not that that's likely to happen, anyway," Geoff went on to explain. "Our figures project that most of the people buying into Saltmarsh Farm will be older, professional, with few school-aged children among them."

Marion should've been angry; Seatham was practically offering the town a bribe. But instead, she sat mesmerized. Geoff looked wonderful on camera. He had such presence. She watched the sunlight flicking over his hair, studied the planes of his handsome face, listened to his deep authoritative voice and wondered how she was ever going to pretend she wanted to divorce this man. This was her husband, her lover, her best friend. She recognized him as such even while that sense of unbridgeable distance returned. It was like watching someone she loved but hadn't seen in a very long time.

Without realizing she was doing it, she lifted an unsteady hand and touched her fingertips to the warm screen. "I'm pregnant, Geoffrey," she whispered. "I've wanted to tell you all day. I'm pregnant."

But the coverage ended, and Geoff's image dissolved. She turned off the TV, picked up her fork, and the silence of her house came washing back.

GEOFF WAS never so glad to be home in his life. Only five days, but they'd seemed like years. He'd missed New England. Missed the trees. Missed old frame houses. Lord, he even begrudged the three hours he'd lost flying across the various time zones, arriving not at five, as his watch still read, but at eight in the evening. He paid the cabdriver, slung his garment bag over his shoulder and took the front steps all in one leap.

It hadn't been the best of trips. He'd heard some news while he'd been gone. Disturbing news. Tiffany was being offered a transfer to the same project, and if he took the job, they'd be working as partners. Why hadn't anybody mentioned this to him? Why hadn't she? She must've known. What really bothered him, though, was the suspicion that Tiffany had inadvertently told Marion.

This idea had hit him last night. He hadn't been able to get Marion's odd behavior off his mind, and finally there it was: Tiffany had probably told her. Not only about her own job offer but about his, as well. Marion's mood had changed so abruptly after seeing Tiffany at the Bridge Street Café, it seemed logical to assume that was the case. What he'd mistaken for indifference had really been anger over the fact that he hadn't told her himself.

Geoff didn't know what he was going to do about the hole he'd dug himself into, but oddly he felt hopeful. Marion might be angry, but at least that meant she cared.

He found her in the dining room, simultaneously talking on the phone, which was tucked in the crook of her shoulder, and washing a window. She was wearing fringed denim shorts and a tie-front sleeveless blouse, her honey-colored hair up in pigtails.

When she heard him come in, she turned, and Geoff knew in that instant there was more to his urge to come home than he'd let himself admit.

"Hi." She smiled shyly.

"Hi." Geoff swore time rolled back. Not only did she look as young as the day he'd first met her, but suddenly he longed to go to her, take her in his arms and kiss her the way he would have years ago after a trip. And for a moment he thought she looked as if that was exactly what she wanted, too.

But the moment passed in a heartbeat. With a blink of an eye and a toss of her head, reality returned.

"I have to go now, Juliana. Geoff's just come home." She dropped her wash rag into a bucket and took hold of the receiver. "Thanks for your help, and I will be in touch. 'Bye."

She hung up and turned. "How was your trip?" she asked with crisp politeness, her gaze not really focused when she looked at him.

"Okay." He tried not to feel dismayed. After all, nothing had changed for her.

"Just okay?" A pulse beat at her temple.

"Yes. I got everything done I had to." He looked around the room. Curtains were down, furniture pushed out of place. "What's going on?"

"Oh, just getting the house ready for the reception."

"Marion, I don't think anybody's going to care whether the windows are washed or not." He draped his garment bag over a chair.

"I know."

"I know you know, but you're going to scour the house, anyway, aren't you?"

She shrugged.

"Can't Mrs. Souza do this?" he asked, referring to the woman who came in to clean twice a week.

"Oh, she's helping. But there's so much to do." Marion went back to her window cleaning. "So, what did you do on your trip?" she asked, scrubbing with unusual vigor.

"Not much really. Some legal work. Lots of wining and dining with people I could've done without. Marion, I've been traveling all day, sitting in airports. I really don't want to talk about work right now."

"Fine," she said, biting off the word.

Her reaction pretty much convinced him he was right; she knew about the job offer and was stewing over his not telling her. His heart lifted. He pulled out a chair and sprawled tiredly. "Was that Juliana Van Bassen on the phone just now?"

"Uh-huh." He waited, but she added nothing more.

"Wedding business?" he persisted.

"Yes." Silence again, but then she offered, "I called to see if she could do the flowers, but she has two other weddings that day. So she referred me to somebody who's just starting up a floral business."

"Oh, that's too bad. The Van Bassen sisters are really good, aren't they?"

She hesitated, eyeing him over her shoulder. He guessed they'd fallen out of the habit of gabbing like this. "They're the best," she replied. "If it was just a matter of a few centerpieces for the tables, I wouldn't mind, but we've got a whole tent to decorate, Geoff. A whole big empty tent. I was really hoping to do something special." She finished drying the window and turned. "Juliana had some suggestions, though, and she's offered me free use of her props—you know, potted trees, lights, that sort of thing." She paused, chewing on her lower lip, darting speculative looks his way. "Are you hungry?"

"Starved."

"There's some leftover chicken in the fridge."

"I can get it," he said, but she went into the kitchen, anyway. This surprised him. They'd fallen into such irregular hours, he'd become used to fending for himself. While he poured himself a tall glass of ale, she made up a plate and slipped it into the microwave.

He'd noticed she'd relaxed somewhat while she'd been talking about the wedding. "How are the rest of the arrangements coming?"

She made a so-so motion with her head that set her pigtails swinging. "Not bad. We don't have a band yet. That's the worst news. On the other hand, the Silvas can cater for us."

"There you go. I'm sure the food'll be so good our guests won't even notice there's no music."

"Don't count on it." She leaned against the counter, ankles crossed, her hands splayed and moving in slow circles across her abdomen.

Geoff frowned. "Your stomach still bothering you?"

She dropped her hands abruptly. "Oh, uh, no. No, I... no." She shook her head, her color heightening a little. The microwave beeped and she hurried to remove the plate.

"If you don't mind, I've got some, uh, some curtains to iron. Okay?"

Geoff watched her hurry off to the laundry room, wondering what he'd done now. Would he ever understand what made that woman tick?

Left to eat alone, he opened one of the newspapers that had accumulated while he'd been away.

Marion was just coming back from the laundry, curtains neatly draped over one arm, when he saw the article. He was sure his eyes popped out of his head, and then he let out an ungracious—considering she was in the room—whoop of victory.

"The Building Commission's ready to cave in? I don't believe it!"

"Swine!" she cursed as she passed him.

"Who? Me or them?"

"Both," she called from the dining room. "You're all swine."

His spirits lifted again, which was a very odd thing to have happen when you were being called a swine, but instinctively he knew she wasn't really insulting him. In fact, her voice held an intriguing note of flirtatiousness.

"You're a fine one to talk," he said, following her into the dining room. "You think I didn't notice those half-page propaganda ads the Conservation Commission ran? Think I didn't see your name listed as one of the sponsors?" For no reason he could fathom, he swatted her shapely derriere with the folded newspaper. It was something he would have done a few years ago, but not now.

He held his breath, waiting for her response, expecting it to be anger. But she only shook her head in mock disparagement, a bewitching little smile playing over her mouth. His heart expanded. Maybe five days' absence had made her miss him, too.

"How are you coming along with Robyn and Nate's rings?" he asked, helping her thread a brass rod through a curtain pocket.

She brightened. "Would you like to see?"

"I'd love to." He followed her into her studio, the amazing thought swirling through his mind: *We're almost having a normal conversation.*

She showed him the rough gold circle that would eventually be Nate's band. Although she said it wasn't a difficult design—a modified copy of an Italian Renaissance ring—it looked pretty intricate to him.

"It's—" he lifted his shoulders "—beautiful."

"You really think so?" She seemed pleased.

"Yes. Of course I do." Encouraged, he turned to look for other works in progress to praise, but his gaze fell, instead, on a large paperback book sitting on her worktable. "What's this?" he asked. He picked it up, scanned the cover and suddenly felt he'd been dropped down an elevator shaft. The title of the book was *How to Negotiate Your Own Divorce.*

MARION FLINCHED. She hadn't meant to leave that book lying around. She'd only wanted to learn more about divorce, about the law, the legal jargon, so she wouldn't sound like a complete ignoramus when she brought up the subject with her husband.

"Never mind," Geoff said, hurling the book down. "I can see what it is."

His reaction startled her. "Why are you so upset? You can't pretend we were never going to get around to the subject, right?" Her stomach hadn't been bothering her before, but it sure was now.

Geoff didn't answer, tightly pressed lips his only reaction. Oh, this was a lot harder than she'd thought. For days she'd been playing out this evening in her mind, how she'd jump right into the subject as soon as he got home, how calm and forthright she'd be. In her mind, oh, yes, she was going to be the epitome of grace in the face of defeat.

Except that no sooner had her eyes met his tonight than her composure had begun to unravel—to say nothing of her intentions. She'd tried to hang on, tried to pretend indifference, but Geoffrey Kent simply proved too much for her. The more she'd fallen under his spell, the harder it was to remember why she needed to discuss divorce.

But with the slamming down of that book, everything was firmly back in place.

"I bought the book thinking we might be able to do the divorce ourselves, you and me together, without involving other lawyers." Her mouth was as dry as dust. "That way, we could keep the entire proceeding a secret, maybe for several months." She wrung her fingers. Her voice wobbled. "I figured you could go off to your new job in California and I could simply say you're away on business. Of course, that story will last just so long before people realize you're not coming back, but at least it'll give the chapel legend a few more months of untarnished life."

Geoff seemed to have stopped breathing sometime while she'd been talking. Now he turned to the window and stood staring out. "How'd you find out about the job offer?" His voice was ominously calm.

Suddenly Marion realized what she'd done. She hadn't meant to let slip the fact that she knew. She'd wanted to wait, to see how long it took him to tell her.

"How'd you find out, Marion?"

"Tiffany," she admitted. "By accident. She mentioned it thinking you'd already told me."

"And you couldn't wait." He spun around to face her. "You immediately had to run out and buy a book."

"Of course I can wait. I *assumed* we would, at least until the wedding was over. We both have too much to do before then. I simply thought you'd feel better if we got the word 'divorce' out in the open."

He gazed at her incredulously and then shook his head, laughing. But in all the days, in all the years that she'd known him, never had Marion heard him laugh in quite that way.

"Where are you going?" she asked, seeing him head for the door.

"I don't know." He was still shaking his head and laughing that cold hurt empty laugh. "I don't know." He strode out into the deepening night, got into his car and drove away.

CHAPTER EIGHT

THE NEXT DAY at noon Geoff stormed into the house, carrying a large cardboard carton. "You want books about divorce? Here. Have a ball." With an angry thrust, the contents of the box thundered to the floor of Marion's studio.

She gaped at the pile, then up at him, stupefied.

"And while you're at it, here are all the forms you'll need to get the divorce process started." He slapped a manila envelope on her bench. "Why wait till after the wedding? Start now."

Before she could utter a single word he was gone again.

Geoff remained in his mood the rest of the week, staying away from the house fourteen, fifteen hours a day. The few minutes they did share together passed in dismal silence.

Marion tried to ignore him. She had jewelry orders to fill, a store to run and wedding preparations to make. In addition, the special town meeting was fast approaching, and there were emergency sessions of the Open Space Committee to attend, letters to the editor that needed writing and one last-ditch visit to Hannah Borden to try to convince her to take the farm off the market. The visit did nothing but raise Hannah's wrath.

Above and beyond all this, Marion was pregnant. She might not carry the baby long, but while she did, she was determined to take good care of it. She had to remember to take her vitamins, eat well and follow her doctor's advice about relaxing. The last thing she needed was a brooding worrisome husband.

Marion tried to ignore him, tried to tell herself she didn't care. Not speaking would simply make their enforced time together pass that much faster. But her efforts didn't work. Geoff was on her mind constantly. No matter what she did, thoughts of him consumed her.

Apparently she'd been wrong to assume he'd feel better with the subject of divorce out in the open. He was really upset. What she didn't understand was why.

Was it that book she'd bought? she wondered as she roamed the local stationery store, shopping for tissue wedding bells. Did he think she was somehow trying to get the legal jump on him? The idea was ludicrous. Geoff knew divorce law inside out. Besides, she'd said quite clearly she thought they could negotiate the divorce *together.*

Most likely, she decided while tacking an Open Space flyer to the message board outside the post office, he was angry because she'd found out about the California job offer before he'd wanted her to. He'd probably hoped to keep that, and the depth of his involvement with Tiffany, a secret until they were legally separated. He might even be thinking she'd use the information against him in court as proof of infidelity—which until this moment hadn't even crossed her mind.

Or was it the suddenness? she asked herself, standing in a daze outside the grocery market. Had that book just caught him off guard? She had to admit she would've been knocked for a loop herself. As angry as she was, she hated the idea of hurting Geoff. Was that what she'd done?

Still, did that justify his dumping all those books in her studio? Scaring her with how wild he'd looked? She'd been a wreck the rest of the day.

Marion was so engrossed in her thoughts she didn't even see the market door open and Bronwyn stepping out.

"Earth to Marion." Bronwyn laughed.

Marion blinked, glanced up and wanted to sink through the sidewalk. Two full weeks had passed since they'd spoken.

Bronwyn adjusted her brown paper sack, her eyes as direct as ever. "Hi. How've you been?" If she was still angry or hurt, she certainly wasn't showing it.

"Busy."

"I can imagine. Weddings are such complicated things to organize. How's it coming?" Bronwyn asked graciously, despite the affront Marion had dealt her by not going through Weddings, Inc.

"It's. . . shaping up. We've decided to have the reception at the house." Her eyes avoided her friend's. Bronwyn had an uncanny knack for reading people, and the last thing Marion wanted her to know was how much trouble she'd had searching for a location.

"Were you able to rent a tent?"

"Yes."

"Great. At this time of year, that isn't always easy."

Don't I know it, Marion thought.

"And music? Have you hired a band, or does Robyn prefer a disc jockey? So many couples these days would rather do that."

Marion wondered how Bronwyn knew to zero in on the detail where she'd had the most difficulty. In fact, with one week to go, she was on the edge of panic.

"Um. . . I'm following a couple of leads." What she couldn't bring herself to admit was that those leads were a seventeen-year-old boy with a boom box and an alarmingly large collection of rap music, and a plump apple-cheeked woman with an accordion and a foot-pedal drum.

"I'm sure something will come through for you."

I'm such a jerk, Marion lamented. *I don't deserve such a friend.*

"Well, I'll leave you to your shopping." Bronwyn started to walk away.

"Bron?" Marion called on a sudden impulse.

She turned. "Yes?"

"I'm sorry about the other day."

Bronwyn smiled. "I know."

"I shouldn't have said the things I did about the chapel and the legend." *Even though I still believe them.*

"No need to apologize. Considering what's been happening in your life, a little anger is perfectly normal."

An enormous weight seemed to lift off Marion's shoulders.

Bronwyn stepped closer. "Do I dare ask how things are going?"

Marion gnawed on her lower lip. How much had changed in two weeks. Geoff was moving to California—and she was pregnant! "About the same," she answered.

"Then, you and Geoff haven't used this time to settle any differences?"

"No." She shook her head. "No."

Bronwyn looked frustrated and corked up with advice, but all she said was, "I wish there was something I could do."

They said goodbye again, but as Bronwyn walked toward her car, she called back, "Hey, Marion? If you need any help with the wedding..." The offer hung in the morning sunshine, waiting.

Marion hesitated, then chucked her pride aside. "Can you find me a good band?"

Bronwyn smiled from ear to ear. "I'll call you tonight."

THE WEATHER TURNED unbearably hot that week. High nineties during the day, lowering only to the high seventies at night. Sitting in his air-conditioned office on Saturday afternoon, Geoff couldn't get his mind off Marion. When he'd left the house that morning, she'd already been outside trimming the lawn.

He'd asked what she was doing, and she'd said, "What does it look like I'm doing?" They'd been sniping for days.

But maybe he'd deserved it. Actually what he'd said was, "What the hell are you doing?"

"Hey!"

Geoff jumped. He'd been so absorbed in his thoughts he hadn't heard anyone coming up the stairs.

"Is this what you do all day?" Graham leaned in the door.

Geoff lowered his feet from his desk. "Caught me."

Graham stepped into the book-lined room. "Just came by to deliver my RSVP for the wedding."

Geoff took the reply and slipped it into his shirt pocket. "Don't rush off. My last client left a few minutes ago."

"Thanks. It's like a sauna out there." Graham flopped onto the leather couch.

"Yes it is. Would you believe Marion's doing yard work today?" Dammit, couldn't he even talk about the weather without bringing his wife into it?

"Is she?" Graham studied his fingernails. "So...how's it going?"

Small knots of anger tightened in Geoff's neck. "Not so good."

"Anything you care to talk about?"

"No." Geoff shook his head, then hauled himself up and began pacing. "I don't know. Damn!" As he paced he twisted his right fist into his left palm. He paused abruptly. "Do you have any idea what Marion did to me this week?" And before he realized it, he was relaying how he'd found the book on divorce. "I felt I'd been sucker-punched."

Graham had been listening so patiently Geoff was surprised when he finally spoke. "Why do you suppose she did a thing like that?"

Geoff's laugh was scornful. "She said she thought I'd feel better discussing the subject." He shook his head, still incredulous, still hurting. "Bottom line is, she can't wait to get me out of her life."

"And how did you come to that conclusion?"

"Long story."

"I'm not going anywhere."

Geoff sighed. "Okay, truth is, I didn't tell her about the job offer I got from Seatham, but she found out, anyway."

"Nice move. Was she mad?"

"I wish."

"Hurt?"

"Huh! That would've meant she cared. No, Marion wasn't mad or hurt. She heard about the job offer and immediately thought, Great. He's half out the door. Let's start talking divorce."

"She assumed you're going to take the job?"

"Mm. Wishful thinking, I'm sure."

"Are you?"

"I don't know," Geoff answered irritably. "I was leaning away from it, but now... I don't know." He turned to look out the window toward Marion's store, missing her. That was the craziest part of all this; the angrier he got at her, the more he missed her.

"Tell me something, how did she find out?"

"About the job? Tiffany."

Graham swore quietly. "I told you that woman was trouble."

"No, no. It was purely an accident. Tiff thought I'd already spoken with Marion." That was the truth. It was. And the fact that Geoff felt disinclined to mention that Tiffany was being offered a job in California, too, held no significance.

"And you don't see any connection?"

"No. I flew back thinking there might be one. But, no. It didn't matter who delivered the news. Marion just latches onto anything these days to push me a little farther out the door."

Graham shook his head. "Tell me, pal, what've you done lately to stop her?"

The room fell quiet, Geoff gazing out the window, Graham's stare drilling into the back of his head. He said he'd felt sucker-punched when he'd found that book, but he'd gone and sucker-punched Marion right back, hadn't he?

"Go home, pal." Graham got up from the sofa and started for the door. "Be nice to that lady of yours. You know you want to."

Geoff only nodded. He felt very confused.

MARION PUSHED DOWN her garden glove and frowned at her watch. "What are you doing home so early?"

"What time is it?" Geoff asked, striding across the front lawn.

"Three."

"I always get home around three on Saturdays."

True, she thought, but considering his behavior lately, she hadn't expected to see him until late that evening, if at all.

"What are you doing?" he asked.

Marion looked at him askance. He still held his head at an aloof angle, still didn't look at her when he spoke, but his tone was civil. She'd become so used to his angry silences she didn't know how to respond. "The tent's coming on Wednesday," she answered simply. "I can't wait for cooler weather. The yard needs doing now."

Geoff tugged off his tie. "Why's the tent coming so early?" He seemed to want to talk and yet keep his distance at the same time.

"You really want to know?"

"Uh-huh."

Still eyeing him warily, she said, "Putting it up takes time, and time's going to be in short supply the rest of the week. I have tons of decorating to do. The caterer will be here setting up tables and chairs. Relatives will be flying in..."

Geoff's dark penetrating eyes were moving over her, and Marion wondered disgustedly why she'd bothered to put on mascara. In this heat and humidity she probably looked like a raccoon right now.

"I'll be out as soon as I've changed," he said.

"You're going to help?"

"Yes. We're in this wedding thing together, aren't we?" Geoff sighed, becoming serious. "Marion, I'm sorry I've left you with most of the wedding preparations until now." His seriousness deepened into a frown. "What's happening with our marriage shouldn't matter. We have this affair to pull off, and somehow we've got to find a way to cooperate."

Marion looked aside. "You're right."

"Okay, glad you agree." He took a deep breath. "Now, stop pushing that mower and go concentrate on your flower beds. I never know what's a plant and what's a weed."

For the first time in a week, Marion smiled. "You *are* a disaster in a garden."

"Thanks." He rapped her nose with his tie and bounded up the front steps, leaving her with more conflicted feelings than she knew what to do with.

Geoff spent the rest of the day mowing, clipping hedges and driving to the garden center for bales of peat moss and other heavy supplies that Marion needed. He welcomed the physical activity, even in the oppressive heat. Racquetball and exercise equipment just weren't doing anything for him these days. He enjoyed being able to breathe fresh air, to hear the river rushing along, feel the sun on his shirtless back—and look up and see Marion just a few feet away.

On hands and knees in a bed of flowers, Marion looked, well, adorable. She was wearing her sun hat, but a fine sprinkling of freckles had blossomed on her cheeks, anyway. She abhorred her freckles, but he'd always rather liked them. In fact, one day he'd called them sexy. "Freckles are a lot of things, Geoffrey, but they are not sexy." He smiled a little, still hearing her indignant voice.

They didn't talk much as they weeded and clipped, not about their personal problems, anyway. He guessed they both preferred avoiding the subject of divorce for now, although he never quite forgot it. Occasionally she chatted on about the wedding, and for a while they even discussed the upcoming town meeting. But for long stretches of time, they just worked, listened to the birds and the river and worked. Maybe it was enough.

Marion reached forward to loosen the soil at the back of the border and her shorts rode high up her thighs. Her legs were long, firm and sleek with perspiration. Under her form-fitting tank top, her breasts swayed with the motion of her digging. He thought they looked fuller these days, but maybe it was just his imagination.

Geoff resumed sawing through a dead branch on one of their oaks, sawing perhaps with more vigor than was necessary. It was a very hot day indeed.

THE HEAT CONTINUED to press down on Eternity through the night. Marion tossed from one side of her bed to the other, trying to find a cool spot. The sheets tangled, her hair matted, her emotions frayed.

Through the open window came the insistent susurration of crickets and cicadas—heat bugs even at night. She tried to concentrate on the tasks that faced her tomorrow but found concentration impossible. The deep croak of a bullfrog who lived in her lily pond continually intruded. He played a delightful bass counterpoint to the high strident singing of the crickets and cicadas and the random tuneful ting of a wind chime.

Marion flung herself onto her back, legs and arms sprawled. Summer was too sensuous, she thought, breathing in the thick sweet fragrance rising from her gardens. Even the heat seemed to take on body, curling around her like a warm cat. And over it all was the soft sibilant slide of the river.

From down the hall came the angry squeak of bedsprings, the thump of a headboard against a wall.

Marion stared at the faintly luminous canopy over her bed but saw Geoff, instead. Geoff working in the yard, sun gleaming off his muscle-rippled back, snug denim jeans hugging powerful legs, masculine appeal in every move he made....

She flung herself to her side. It was two in the morning and she hadn't slept a wink. What was worse, Geoff seemed to be just as awake and restless. The heat was the culprit, this stifling stillness and the heat. She should've given in and let him install air-conditioning when he'd suggested it. It didn't matter that New England got only a handful of nights like this one. When one of those nights was upon you, all the others became meaningless.

Her hand drifted from her hot forehead to her sticky neck, over one breast and down to her belly. Every inch of her pulsed responsively. Without a doubt, summer was too sensuous. She closed her eyes and summoned a dream of deep winter.

IN MARION'S OPINION, Monday arrived much too soon. She wasn't looking forward to the town meeting. Not one bit. Anticipation had been building for weeks, and she really didn't want to be around when the lid blew.

Basically she didn't like controversy. Certainly she cared about issues and held strong opinions, but when it came to public debate she felt like the proverbial duck out of water, and as she entered the high school that evening, heading right into the fray, she wondered if she shouldn't have her head examined.

"Good evening, Marion," a woman at the door said. "Let's get your name checked off," she murmured, running her finger down a list of voters. She made a mark, then handed Marion a packet of information.

"Thank you." Marion smiled nervously and slipped into the noisy auditorium. The seats were arranged in three sections. The Open Space Committee was sitting up front in the section to the right. With her stomach jumping worse than ever, she joined them.

"Did you see yesterday's editorial?" a woman named Bev inquired, her eyes gleaming.

"Yes, I did," Marion said distractedly. The fact that the regional newspaper had come out against Seatham was a major coup, and when she'd seen the editorial yesterday at breakfast, she'd crowed rather smugly. When she'd handed the paper to Geoff, he'd sworn; words had come out of his mouth she'd never heard him use before. The memory still made her smile.

With a start she realized he was already here, standing up front with Seatham people. Her smile deepened all the way to her heart.

Which made absolutely no sense. Nothing had changed between them, and the fact that the weekend had passed rather pleasantly was merely a quirk.

Geoff looked up and met her gaze and, oh, Lord, there went her heart rate. He nodded hello, and she wondered, *What've we done, Geoffrey? How have we landed in this mess?* She longed for the days when they came to town meetings together, sat together, voted together, occasionally disagreeing, but never like this.

But those days were gone, weren't they?

With an effort she turned her attention to the other Seatham people. She recognized the chief architect of the project, a financial analyst, an environmental engineer, various executives and, of course, Tiffany.

Marion's features hardened. She didn't want to hate the woman, but Lord, how could she not? Tiffany was gorgeous, she was brilliant and she had Geoff.

With a start, she realized Geoff was still watching her. He glanced at Tiffany, then turned again to Marion, frowning. Feeling her color heighten, Marion opened the information packet and buried her nose in material she hadn't the vaguest desire to read.

Behind her the auditorium was quickly filling, the noise level rising. On stage the board of selectmen now took their seats at a table to the right, the finance committee to the left, with the town-meeting moderator at his podium in the middle. Large floor fans whirred, stirring the muggy air.

The moderator began to rap his gavel and slowly order descended on the gathering. He was an affable man whose sense of humor was often needed and appreciated during heated debates.

The minister of the First Meetinghouse led them in prayer, followed by the Pledge of Allegiance. With ceremonies ended, the moderator then defined the issue the townspeople would be asked to vote on.

On the surface it seemed a simple matter—amendments to the zoning laws. One issue, one vote. But everyone knew what that simple vote meant. If the changes passed, Seatham's project would be able to move forward. If they didn't, Seatham might as well pack up and go home tonight. No one expected to be out of here anytime soon.

The Seatham vice president in charge of the Eternity project was the first to stand up. He took a microphone and addressed the gathering from the floor of the auditorium. Marion listened to his speech about Seatham's twenty-year track record of building quality developments, but she knew it was all just introductory hype.

When he handed over the floor to Geoff and the architect, she felt the auditorium settle in, recognizing this as the real start of business. In spite of her adversarial stand, she filled with pride.

Geoff asked for the lights to be dimmed, then for the next fifteen minutes he and the architect led everyone through a slide presentation that included several aerial photos and topographical maps, as well as detailed sketches of the proposed facilities.

As soon as the presentation ended, hands went up. Teenagers, working as microphone runners, were kept busy dashing up and down the aisles. The moderator repeated questions and deftly directed them to the appropriate people. Sometimes that was a selectman, sometimes a Seatham executive; most often it was Geoff.

Meanwhile, Marion and her Open Space Committee sat quietly on the sidelines. They weren't really involved in issues such as building heights, road widenings or fire district expansion. But Marion knew their moment would come.

Finally someone asked what Seatham intended to do with the two hundred acres of woods that stretched west of the proposed building site. She and her colleagues exchanged glances.

The moderator gazed down at the front row. "Geoff? Or anyone." His preference was obvious.

For one unfathomable moment, Marion thought she sensed hesitancy in her husband. Something in the set of his shoulders. But he got to his feet and turned on the projector, clicking back to an aerial view that encompassed the entire farm.

"As we explained earlier, all the proposed housing units will be clustered within this circle." He outlined the area with a long wooden pointer. "With the pool and gym here—" the pointer moved "—and the tennis courts here. All the rest—" the pointer swept across the woodlands "—will be left untouched, except for a carefully planned system of walking paths and bike trails."

He paused and Marion noticed that Tiffany was calling him over. He leaned toward her and she whispered in his ear. Marion clenched her fists, clenched her jaw, clenched just about every part of her, remembering the newspaper photograph of them in a similar pose.

"Incidentally, those paths," Geoff continued smoothly, "will be open to the general public, free of charge."

Marion winced. This was news, welcome news from the sound of the murmurs she heard rising from the crowd.

Immediately the chairman of the Open Space Committee, a young lawyer just a year out of law school, raised his hand. "This sounds wonderful," he said with just the right touch of sarcasm. "Bike paths, clustered housing. But tell me, what guarantee do we have that Seatham will never develop that wooded land? Once the area's rezoned, what's to stop you from expanding your original plan and building all over the farm?"

Curiously, Marion noticed Geoff hand the mike to the finance director.

"It simply wouldn't be in our best interests to do that." The finance director then went on to explain the folly of overbuilding—quite convincingly, too, Marion thought.

"But that still doesn't answer my question," the young lawyer said. "What *guarantee* do we have that you'll leave that land undeveloped?"

Again, Geoff eased back, and the job of answering fell to the environmental engineer.

"Conservation laws strictly regulate our movement on that piece of property. Your existing laws will be your guarantee."

"Yes, and they're wonderful laws, but they only apply to the wetlands. What about the woods?"

For the first time that evening Tiffany stood up and quickly introduced herself. Her voice was authoritative, her appearance stunning, her attitude almost bored—as if she was growing impatient with these voters' inability to see the obvious. "As the corporate attorney representing Seatham, I've been authorized to add a written clause to our general proposal stating that we will not, underline not, develop that land now or in the future." And turning to the young lawyer standing beside Marion, she asked, "Does that answer your question?"

Marion noticed the tips of his ears turn pink as he nodded. Along the row, her colleagues sat back, somewhat confused.

Marion was scowling right along with them when a thought entered her mind, a terrible thought that she tried to ignore. She didn't like speaking out at town meetings, but it didn't look like the idea was occurring to anyone else.

With a feeling of profound anxiety, she raised her hand.

"Marion." Wearing the tiniest of grins, the moderator called on her.

She hauled herself up two-handedly, using the seat in front for support. "My question is, do we also have a guarantee that Seatham won't ever sell those woodlands? To another developer, for instance?"

Her legs gave way and she dropped back into her seat, while a loud buzz of consternation arose. It was nothing, though, compared to the look of malice in Tiffany's eyes.

Marion became aware of Geoff's attention, his eyes racing from her to Tiffany, and before Tiffany could utter whatever was on her mind, he got to his feet and took her microphone.

"Unfortunately we haven't been authorized to offer such a guarantee." His eyes were fixed on the moderator. "That's only because the scenario just presented has never occurred to anyone at Seatham. I hope the town would see this as a further sign of Seatham's goodwill." His voice dropped as if that was the end of the argument.

Marion's cheeks burned. She'd feared this would happen. All along she'd feared it would ultimately come down to her and him.

She was on her feet without knowing how she got there. "But the fact remains there's no written guarantee, right?"

Geoff turned, his exasperated gaze meeting hers, and in that moment she sensed he was weighing sides. Her against Seatham and Tiffany.

He blinked, looked away and then launched into a dazzling recitation of real-estate law, full of legal jargon and mention of precedent-setting cases. It took Marion a while but eventually she realized what he was doing. He was building a case that exempted and protected Seatham from having to make such a promise. It all sounded very reasoned and reasonable, and even before he was done Marion knew the voters were swayed.

The moderator scanned the crowd. "Are there any other questions? Any comments or opinions?"

Marion's hand went up yet again. He grinned as he acknowledged her.

Incensed by the condescension she read in his attitude, she squared her shoulders and let her anger give her strength. "Yes, speaking for the Open Space Committee, I have a few comments. I'm sure everyone is acquainted with our position already, but I'd feel remiss if I didn't repeat it, anyway.

"One of the mandates of our committee is to protect unspoiled areas of this town and preserve its character. In my opinion Seatham presents the largest threat to that ideal we've ever faced. While Seatham has presented us with a very attractive development, we have to remember that it *is* a development, and no one here can honestly say that area will ever be the same again once it's been developed." She flinched, hearing herself go around in circles.

"At the same time we have to remember we're not totally certain about some of Seatham's claims. The sewage system, for instance. Will it really protect our marshlands?

"But the biggest uncertainty of all is whether Seatham will preserve the woods, as they now claim, or decide to sell them later. If they're so pure of heart, why can't they give us a guarantee? What's the big deal?

"After we've cast our vote, there'll be no turning back. Once the trees and marshes are gone, there'll be no good in saying we made a mistake. The time to check the mistake is now."

When she sat down, there was a smattering of applause, which grew loud and approving. The moderator raised his hand for quiet, then pointed to the back of the auditorium. "Yes, Hannah?"

Marion swung around to see iron-jawed sixty-year-old Hannah Borden lumbering to her feet. Hannah started talking without the microphone.

"Hold on, Ms. Borden. We don't want to miss anything you have to say." Suppressed laughter rippled through the auditorium. Hannah Borden was notorious for saying exactly what was on her mind, decorum and parliamentary procedure be damned.

"I haven't said anything all night, seeing as how this issue involves my land and all, but it's been damn hard. For one thing, what me and my family does with our farm is nobody's business, and what we want to do is sell. I don't appreciate our private affairs becoming a public circus, and what I especially don't appreciate is opposition from people I used to consider neighbors. I think certain people ought to have more respect and mind their own business, to say nothing of minding their husbands."

A burst of incredulous gasps mixed with outright laughter.

"Thank you, Hannah." The moderator cut her off, even though she was still on her feet. "Geoff?" he said quickly.

Geoff got up, looked at Hannah Borden, scanned the crowd, and his scowl silenced them all. "Whatever the outcome of this vote, I want to remind everyone that difference of opinion is what town meetings are all about, and although my wife and I don't see eye to eye on this issue, I respect her right to disagree. If I can accept that, so should everyone else." He sat down to another round of applause.

For what? Marion wondered. Democracy in general? The debate was clearly disintegrating. The moderator seemed to think so, too.

He asked if there were any other comments, and when only three seconds of silence had passed, he quickly said, "It seems we're ready to vote." He adjusted his spectacles, explained the warrant again, then intoned, "All in favor?"

Marion crossed her fingers, while counters moved up the aisle, earnestly tallying the number of raised hands.

"All opposed?"

Marion raised her hand.

Finally all the numbers were in. "The vote, ladies and gentlemen..."

Marion closed her eyes and prayed.

"...is 348 in favor, 321 against. The motion carries." The moderator banged his gavel although no one heard amid the upswell of reaction.

Marion's heart plummeted. All around her, voices murmured, "Oh, no!" and, "So close!" Meanwhile the Seatham contingent were on their feet, shaking hands and clapping each other's backs, even while the moderator was calling for someone to motion for an adjournment. Geoff, she noticed, simply gathered up papers.

"Marion, do you want to go out for a drink?" someone to her right asked.

"No thanks."

"Are you sure?"

"Yes."

"See you at the next meeting, then."

Marion didn't answer. Just picked up her purse and quietly slipped out a side door.

CHAPTER NINE

GEOFF KNEW Marion was home. Her truck was in the driveway, but he couldn't find her anywhere in the house. Finally he looked out a back window and noticed a pale glimmer of clothing down by the river. Loosening his tie, he crossed the lawn to join her.

She had to know he was there, yet she refused to turn around. Geoff eased himself into the hammock that hung between two trees and gazed up at the murky night sky. Neither of them spoke. Just listened to the river sliding by. Consummately aware of each other.

When Geoff could take the silence no longer, he asked, "How're you doing?"

"I'll live," she replied, flicking a pebble into the water. Streamers of light from the opposite shore fragmented. "How come you're not out celebrating?"

"When I can be home with you?"

She shot him a dark look over her shoulder.

"Didn't feel like it." The others had gone. They'd tried to badger him into going, too. Tiffany had even become petulant. But he'd never felt the need to get home so urgently before.

"Are you ever going to speak to me again?" he asked.

"Probably not."

Geoff placed his hands under his head for a pillow and smiled sadly. Despite Marion's flippancy, there were tears in her voice.

"I don't know why I'm lying here feeling guilty that Seatham won. I've always thought they were bringing the town a great—"

"Why'd you do it, Geoff?" she interrupted.

He knew exactly what she was referring to and didn't try to quibble. "I tried to stay out of it, Marion."

"But you didn't. What I want to know is why."

His sigh came from his toes. "That's what I *do*. Expecting me not to come to the defense of one of my clients would be like asking a fish not to swim."

"Or a shark not to bite?"

"Or a shark not to bite. Although I don't appreciate the comparison. I see it more as an ethical mandate."

"Are you sure that's the only reason?"

"What other could there be?"

Marion lifted her chin. Her profile was limned in light reflected off the water. "Well, seems to me you might've been trying to bail Tiffany out. Did you think she couldn't come up with a proper reply to my question? Were you running to her defense?"

Geoff leaned up on his elbows. "Was I *what?*"

"Or," she went on, her jaw wobbling a little, "were you just trying to prove what a good team player you were to those Seatham stuffed shirts?"

"Dammit, Marion! I wasn't trying to prove any such thing, and I certainly wasn't running to Tiffany's defense."

"Really? So what were you doing?"

"Did it ever cross your mind that maybe I was trying to protect you?"

She swung around. "Protect me? Who from?" When he didn't answer she stepped closer. "Tiffany? You were trying to protect me from Tiffany?"

"Maybe."

"Oh, great. What did you expect? A cat fight?"

"I don't know what I expected. I just didn't want anything awkward to happen."

Marion folded her arms. "Let me get this straight. You made a complete jackass out of me in front of everybody we know in order to protect me?"

"Marion, I did not make a jackass of you. I just answered your question. Simply. Dispassionately."

"You did a legal tap dance," she accused. "It wasn't simple. It wasn't dispassionate."

"Marion, I doubt anyone else shares that opinion."

"Really? Did you take an exit poll?"

Geoff growled deep in his throat. He had to be married to the most frustrating woman on earth. "Tell me, Marion, would you have respected me if I hadn't defended my client?"

"You did that dance on my head so I'd *respect* you?"

"Well, sort of. Did it work?"

She gasped incredulously. "You're impossible!"

Obviously she was in no mood for humor. He lay back and she turned to watch the river again.

"You held your ground well, Marion."

She flicked another pebble into the water. "Yeah, right."

"You did. Your passion for your cause was really moving, and I respect that. I was..." He paused. He'd been about to say he was very proud of her, but she wasn't his to be proud of anymore. "I was touched. Although, quite honestly, I hope we never land on opposite sides of an issue like this again."

She snorted. "It isn't likely. I'm quitting the Open Space Committee and never joining anything again."

"Why, for heaven's sake?"

"It isn't me. I was shaking in my boots every second I was speaking."

Geoff sensed the admission was painful. "I know. All the more reason why I admire you." He rocked his weight to get the hammock swinging. After a while he said, "You know, I'm almost sorry to see this fight come to an end. I've enjoyed running into you at board meetings."

"Oh, sure. It's been a blast."

Geoff sighed. He guessed there wasn't much he could say tonight to appease her. The irony was, though, he *had* enjoyed the competition. He hadn't realized it until this moment, when it was over. Well, maybe not the competition itself—not having Marion on his side had done bizarre things to his sense of well-being—but he'd enjoyed having her involved in an activity that overlapped his work. Now, the only thing left linking them was Robyn's wedding. After Saturday, they'd have nothing.

"Geoff, I really cared about that farm."

The misery in her voice unnerved him, and he wasn't as confident as he could've been when he replied, "Don't worry. The farm's going to be all right."

"You can't guarantee that."

Geoff's breathing came faster. "Maybe I can."

Slowly she turned. "What?"

"I'm only talking about the woodlands now. Quite frankly, I've never had any qualms about Seatham's building plans. But those two hundred acres—I think I can find a way to guarantee they remain undeveloped."

Marion's eyes narrowed. "How?"

He leaned up on his elbows, smiling. "I can tap-dance to all sorts of tunes, Marion. I know lots of steps." He was sure what he was saying would cheer her.

Instead, she came over to the hammock and glared down at him with black outrage in her eyes. "You knew all along they wanted to develop those woods, didn't you?"

He was so stunned he could only stammer. "No, I—"

"Or sell them, which is just as bad. And yet you went right ahead and defended them and made a fool of me in the process. Oooh, you're such a . . . a lawyer!" She shuddered as if being a lawyer was the most contemptible profession on earth. "Tap dance? I'll give you a tap dance."

The next thing Geoff knew, the hammock was flipping over and he was tumbling to the root-gnarled ground.

MARION WAS STILL furious with Geoff the next day, and when she saw him leaving his office at noon, she refused to acknowledge him. She was outside the gown shop, carefully fitting Robyn's bridal dress into the cab of her truck, and as he passed, she simply tossed her chin in the air.

He didn't say anything, either. He was wearing an elastic bandage around his left wrist—a pitiful attempt to convince her he'd been injured in that tumble from the hammock—and as he walked by her he made an exaggerated performance of raising that wrist to look at his watch.

Marion stuffed the gown in, slammed the door and tromped across the street to the shoe store to pick up her dyed-to-order pumps. The clerk who waited on her had been at the town meeting, too—*everybody* Marion ran into today had been at that blasted meeting—and naturally had to bring up the subject, in spite of Marion's obvious embarrassment.

"I'm sorry your side couldn't've won, Marion, but I have to tell you—" the woman clapped a hand over her heart "—that husband of yours is a treasure, the way he stood up and defended your right to dissent. He looked so mad at Hannah Borden I thought she might croak from fright."

This was the third time Marion had heard that sentiment today, and frankly, she was getting sick of it.

Center Jewelers was right next door, and although Marion had scheduled her salesclerks so that she wouldn't have to work the entire week, she decided to pop in, anyway, to see how things were going. While she was at it, maybe she'd sound Lynn out about the meeting.

"Oh, I didn't see it that way at all," Lynn protested after Marion had presented her version of Geoff's speech. "I thought Geoff was quite courteous and objective with you."

Marion had been hearing that opinion all morning, too.

From the jewelry store she drove to the bakery to drop off the cake ornament that had just arrived special delivery from Robyn—a traditional bride and groom made of delicate porcelain—and from the bakery, she drove home.

By then she was beginning to wonder if she was losing her mind. *Had* she overreacted to Geoff's defense of Seatham? True, his words about her right to dissent had been nice, but all in all... No, she still thought he'd done a hatchet job on her. She still had every right to be angry.

As had become her habit, Marion set aside a portion of her afternoon to relax. She went out to a cushioned chaise under an old apple tree, shut her eyes and before long was enjoying a deep tranquillity within. She'd learned to meditate in college, but had stopped when life got too busy—or when she'd *believed* it got too busy. Strange how it took a doctor's order to get her to do something she really enjoyed. After twenty minutes, she lifted her languid eyelids...

And found Geoff sitting in a lawn chair right in front of her. He was watching her, chin propped on a fist. For a moment he seemed to flow with the peace inside her, to be a natural and integral part of it—which surprised her, considering how angry she was with him.

"Did I disturb you?" The chill in his voice reminded her he was equally angry.

"No." She blinked.

"Are you alert?" He was abruptness personified.

Memories of the previous night returned, and all the effects of her meditation vanished. She swung her feet to the ground. "Yes."

"Good, because I don't want to have to repeat this. First, I've never ever thought Seatham was up to anything shady with those two hundred acres." His dark eyes seemed to be shooting sparks. "Second, if you think I did—and I'm sure you did from the lovely names you called me—then you don't know me very well and we're in deeper trouble than I thought. And third," he went on relentlessly, "we're having a wedding here Saturday. I've got to stop in at the office a couple of hours each day, but otherwise I'll be available to help with whatever needs doing. I'd appreciate it if you'd just tell me what that is and leave me alone to do it."

"Fine!" Marion shot back. "But are you sure you'll be able to help—you know, having that terrible injury and all?"

Geoff's expression became thunderous. "Just give me a rundown of what's happening."

Marion leaned over the chaise and snatched up a spiral notebook. Upon straightening, she noticed the swelling in Geoff's wrist. "Omigod." She reached out but he pulled his arm away.

"The schedule, Marion."

She eased back into the chair cushions, somewhat subdued. "Okay." She flipped open the notebook, trying to concentrate. "The tent crew's coming tomorrow. They'll be erecting the tent and unloading tables and chairs."

"Is there anything you want me to do while this is going on?"

"If you don't mind. I need you to run by the Van Bassens' florist shop and fill the truck with all the ficus trees and potted things they can spare. They've put together a few boxes of decorations for me, too."

"Anything else?" he asked, brisk and businesslike.

"Yes. The fish market's lending us a few large coolers for ice and drinks. Could you get those, too?"

"Okay. What else?"

"If you can stand my company," she said with mild sarcasm, "I really need you here to help string lights and arrange tables."

He ignored her tone. "What happens Thursday?"

"More of the same. The caterers will be delivering china and tablecloths and setting up their buffet things. We'll probably still be decorating."

"What about my tux?"

"Friday. When the rest of the men are here, you can all go pick up your tuxes together just in case they need any last-minute alterations."

"When are your parents flying up?"

"Friday. So are the Lloyds. My parents want to rent a car so they can spend next week visiting friends. But Nate's family will need to be met at the airport."

"Do you need me for that?"

Marion was growing weary under Geoff's cool persistent interrogation. She didn't like this cold war they'd fallen into. Over the weekend they'd agreed to shelve personal problems in order to pull this wedding together, but the town meeting had upset everything again.

"No. Nate and Robyn plan to stop at Logan on their way here. They'll be bringing both their cars to fit everybody in."

"Oh? Who's everybody?"

Marion swallowed painfully. She wished they didn't have this rancor between them, especially with the wedding so close. "Nate's parents, his grandmother, his sister and brother-in-law and their two children."

"And all these people are coming here?"

"Yes, but only for the day. They've made reservations to stay at the Haven Inn."

Finally Geoff's steady stream of questions faltered. He tilted his head. "Even Robyn and your parents?"

"Yes."

His eyebrows almost met. "But they usually stay here when they come to visit."

"I know, and I hope they're not hurt. I did invite them to come here first thing Saturday morning, to dress and take pictures."

"Marion, why the devil didn't you...?"

"Think, Geoffrey."

He frowned harder. Within seconds his head snapped up. "Oh."

"Yes, oh."

Neither of them looked at the other, but she knew they had the same thought: where would they sleep if Robyn and her parents stayed over?

Marion chided herself for feeling so uneasy. It wasn't as if their sleeping in the same bed would mean anything—to him, at least.

"Isn't the bridal party supposed to have a rehearsal the night before the wedding?" he asked. She was relieved to find another avenue to take her thoughts down.

"Yes, and after that Nate's parents are hosting a traditional rehearsal dinner."

"Fine, let's move on to D day," he said brusquely.

Marion sighed. "Let's not and say we did."

He leaned forward, flipped the notebook to the page headed Saturday and looked down the interminable list: reminders of hair appointments, flower deliveries, the arrival times of the cake, the photographer, limousine, musicians, the bartender and catering crew.

"Agreed. I'll take it as it comes. Just wind me up and point me in the right direction. Before we get off the subject, though, I have one more question. What band did you end up getting?"

"Would you believe the Honeymooners?"

"You're kidding! How did you manage that? I thought they were booked for another wedding."

"They were, but Bronwyn offered a discount to the couple who'd hired them if they'd accept a different band."

"And they took it?"

"It was a very big discount." Marion realized she was smiling and self-consciously lowered her gaze. "Geoff, listen, I have a few things to say, too. First, I'm sorry you sprained your wrist. I didn't set out deliberately to hurt you. I was just angry. Second, I might have called you a shark and a lawyer—" she placed mocking emphasis on the last word "—but if you think I really believe you're disreputable, then you don't know *me* very well, either. Why would I suggest we negotiate our divorce together, hmm? Rather like putting my head in the shark's mouth, wouldn't you say? And third... Oh, never mind. I've capitulated enough for one day."

The tiniest of smiles was ticking at Geoff's mouth. "Come on, you can't stop there."

She looked aside, huffing. "All right. Thanks for defending my right to dissent. Now can we get on with this wedding with at least the level of civility we reached last weekend?"

Geoff inclined his head. "Of course."

They discussed details of the preparations for a while longer, but finally Geoff got to his feet. "What time do you think this bash will be over?"

"I have no idea." She rose, too. "Depends on how good a time we're having."

Geoff's mouth tightened. A frown had entered his expression again, and Marion realized he probably wasn't looking forward to the wedding as a good time. Even his asking when it would be over was an indication of his eagerness to be gone.

Soon enough, Marion thought. Soon enough. This would be their very last weekend together.

"I'm not sure you want to talk about this now..." she began hesitantly as they walked toward the house.

"When am I leaving?" So, his mind *had* been on the same subject. She nodded.

"Is it all right with you if I don't leave until Sunday?" He determinedly avoided her eyes, his voice taking on a hard edge. "I'd like to at least pack a toothbrush. Or do you want me to hit the road the very minute the wedding's over?"

A painful knot tightened in her throat. "Take as much time as you need. A few days..."

"One's enough." A muscle in his jaw jumped.

"But all your books, your clothes..."

"I'll send a moving company after I'm settled."

Out of nowhere tears were stinging Marion's eyes. She blinked them back furiously. This wasn't what she wanted, but how did you ask someone to stay if he really wanted to go? How *could* you say stay, when leaving was in his best interest?

Her thoughts were growing far too dismal. She forced them back to the wedding. "Do you think we made the right decision?"

Geoff seemed to stop breathing.

"You know," she hastened to explain. "Your moving back here to squash rumors and all."

"Oh, that. Yes, it was the right decision. Think of the alternative, Marion, how upset your folks would've been, how we would've wrecked Robyn's wedding. Yes, we made the right decision. Don't doubt it for a minute."

She chewed her bottom lip. "But do you think we can pull it off? Are we going to convince anyone we're still a happily married couple?"

He didn't answer right away. "I'm not sure, Marion." He shook his head. "I'm really not sure."

His answer worried her more than she cared to admit.

THE NEXT TWO DAYS unfolded almost as Marion had outlined. Almost. What she couldn't have predicted was the rain on Wednesday, which came down so hard that the crew erecting the tent, indomitable though they were, had to occasionally stop and take cover. Consequently everything got backed up.

Another thing Marion hadn't anticipated—a recurrence of the mysterious phone calls that had plagued her last spring. She'd pick up the receiver, say hello, and the caller would instantly hang up. Of course, *Geoff* never got any of these calls. He'd answer and someone would always say hello back. Quite often that someone was Tiffany.

He admitted it openly, and though he claimed the calls were business-related, Marion remained skeptical. He and Tiffany undoubtedly had lots to discuss these days, like living arrangements and travel plans.

She tried to stay out of their way, and for the most part she thought she succeeded. Her days contained enough wedding mayhem to keep her sufficiently distracted, and at night when things settled, she still had her jewelry-designing to fill her sleepless hours.

Yet Marion was well beyond the point where she believed anything would ever fill her life the way Geoff had. She only hoped she'd be able to get through the wedding without breaking down.

LUCKILY GEOFF HAD only one client on Friday morning, and as soon as he'd seen her to the stairs he hurried back to his desk to tidy it up for the weekend. Relatives would be arriving at the house around noon, and he still had wedding chores to do.

In his haste, he knocked over a silver frame, a picture of him and Marion taken four years earlier at a family gathering. Righting it, he discovered the glass had cracked. "Damn," he whispered. He really liked this picture.

His gaze moved over the photograph, from Marion's wide sunny smile to her loving blue eyes. Unexpectedly his throat began to burn.

Living with her these past three weeks had been harder than he'd anticipated. On his body. On his mind. On his soul. Leaving wasn't what he wanted. But how did you say, "Let me stay," when someone really wanted you to go?

And Marion wanted him to go, of that he had no doubt. A couple of days ago she'd already started asking when he was leaving.

She herself was sailing through this ordeal as calm as ever. Meditating. Eating well. Puttering in her studio even after long exhausting days spent on wedding preparations. Nothing ruffled Marion.

Except Tiffany. Marion still got that look in her eye when the phone rang, the look that accused him of being unfaithful. He'd given up trying to convince her otherwise. Marion didn't want to listen. His infidelity was her excuse to say goodbye to a relationship she'd clearly outgrown, and she was going to hang on to that excuse, flimsy as it was, right to the bitter end.

Well, after Sunday, the end wouldn't be long in coming. O'Toole had called twice this week asking if he'd made a decision about the California job. So far Geoff had put him off, but first thing Monday he intended to say yes. Within a week he'd be three thousand miles away.

"Mr. K., what happened?"

Geoff started. "Oh, nothing much, Freddie." He set the frame down as his receptionist walked into the room.

"Let me take that home with me. I'll have it fixed by Monday."

Before Geoff could protest, Freddie had snatched up the frame. She smiled, holding it up. "I know it's none of my business, Mr. K., but I have to tell you, I'm really happy you and your wife are back together."

Geoff felt his heart drop to his shoes. "You... knew I'd moved out?"

"Yeah, I had a hunch."

Geoff felt uneasy. He liked Freddie; she was an efficient and dependable receptionist, but they weren't exactly on terms that allowed for this type of personal conversation.

"You haven't said anything to anyone, I hope? Marion and I have tried to keep that week quiet so Robyn wouldn't find out. No need to get her unnecessarily upset."

Freddie shook her head. "I'm not a gossip—which is why I haven't said anything to you so far about that Ms. Taylor."

After several taut seconds Geoff said, "Go on."

She drew a deep breath. "Well, I'm not sure if you've been aware of the fact, but Ms. Taylor's been after you since you first started working together."

"I've been aware of no such thing, Frederica."

"No surprise. She's a real snake in the grass, that one."

Geoff considered reprimanding his receptionist. She was clearly talking out of line. But his curiosity was stronger than his sense of what was proper.

"First time she dropped by our office she said to me, 'Now there's one gorgeous male,' meaning you."

Geoff tugged on his earlobe, feeling his color deepen.

"And then she started asking me all sorts of questions about you. Personal questions, you know? I answered some, but then I got fed up. I told her you were off limits, you were happily married. But she said no, no you weren't, and she intended to do something about it." Freddie ducked her head, her hair falling forward to conceal her expression.

Waves of self-consciousness flowed through Geoff as he realized his and Marion's discontent had been apparent to those around them.

"A few weeks went by, and one day out of curiosity I had to ask her if was she making any progress with you. Knowing you, naturally I didn't think she was, but I wanted to hear her admit it—which, of course, she'd sooner die than do. I told her again she was chasing the wrong guy, she'd never get to you, you had too much integrity. And you know what she said? She said, 'Freddie, there are lots of ways to split up a couple. If you can't get to one, then you get to the other.' That's exactly what she said."

Geoff's blood ran hot and then icy cold. "When was this?"

"Oh, last April maybe. I'm sorry for not coming to you sooner, but I wasn't sure it was my place. Anyway, I just had to let you know how glad I am she failed. You had me worried there for a while when you moved out. I couldn't imagine what Ms. Taylor had done or if I could've prevented it by warning you."

The whole room seemed to be spinning out of focus, out of control. Geoff thought he heard Freddie's voice, but it came from a very long distance. "What did you say?"

"Do you need me anymore? Are we done here?"

"Oh, uh, yes." He tried to smile. "Take off."

"Thanks, Mr. K. See you at the wedding tomorrow."

After Freddie left, Geoff paced his office for nearly fifteen minutes, trying to get a grip on his thoughts. What the hell had Tiffany been up to all spring? It still seemed impossible. She was so professional. He valued her helpfulness, trusted her judgment. Yet, what would Freddie gain from making up such a story?

On an abrupt thought, Geoff bolted for the door and ran down the stairs. The evening Marion had walked in on him and Tiffany, they'd been working here, downstairs, because Tiff had wanted access to Freddie's computer.

When Marion had come to the door, he'd been leaning his arm on this file cabinet, just so, while Tiffany had been standing there, facing him. Facing the window.

Geoff shook his head. This was crazy. His marriage had been troubled before Tiffany's appearance.

Still, he stepped into Tiffany's spot and just as he'd suspected, it commanded a clear view of the street. She would have seen Marion coming half a block away.

He paced, not wanting to believe the picture that was emerging, but details kept popping into his head uninvited.

Marion had been coming to the office with a package marked Urgent that had been delivered to the house by mistake. In the confusion of the moment, he'd ignored the package. When he'd finally gotten around to it the next day, he'd found it was from Seatham and not really that important at all.

Now a clammy suspicion slithered down his back. He picked up the phone, punched in the number for Seatham Boston and asked for the mail room. After the clerk who answered found the appropriate records, Geoff asked, "And whose office did that package originate from?"

The answer should have surprised him, but it didn't. After all, Graham had warned him three weeks ago, hadn't he? He'd said Tiffany was trouble and he'd been right.

Good Lord, if Tiffany had orchestrated that kiss, what else had she done?

Even while his heart ached for his wife, his spirits lifted. All this time he'd thought Marion was just using Tiffany as an excuse to get out of their marriage. But she'd really been jealous! She'd been hurt, she'd been angry—and jealous!

Geoff laughed out loud, although he recognized that the situation wasn't funny. A lot of damage had been done, and he didn't have a clue how to begin reversing it. He wasn't even sure there was time. But at least now he felt he had a fighting chance.

CHAPTER TEN

FRIDAY NOONTIME, Marion heard the lively tooting of horns in the driveway that announced Robyn and Nate's arrival. She was putting together a pasta salad, spinning about her overcrowded kitchen like a whirling dervish.

"Geoff?" she called through the screen door. He and one of the tent-company workers were crossing the lawn, carrying a heavy wooden panel, one of six, which, when bolted together, would form a dance floor.

"I heard." He lowered the panel to the lawn, the muscles of his back bunching and rippling under his clinging black T-shirt.

Marion scolded herself for stopping to admire, but Lord, how could she not? He'd been parading that remarkable body in her view for the past hour.

She pushed the salad into the already crammed refrigerator and flew out the door. Geoff met her at the bottom of the porch steps.

"What a way to meet people for the first time!" She gazed at the chaos in the yard while smoothing her hair. But her biggest concern was not the physical mess but rather knowing that the event that had precipitated Geoff's moving back was finally upon them. She still wasn't sure they were going to pull it off.

"Well, this is it." She sighed worriedly.

"Mmm. Show time." Geoff smiled in a way that baffled her. "Here, take my hand. It's what they'll be expecting."

Robyn rushed up the driveway and flung herself into Geoff's arms. "Do you realize I haven't seen you since Easter!"

"Hi, shortcake." He laughed, lifting her off her feet in an exuberant hug.

Marion looked on, unexpectedly aching for the ability to do what her sister was doing, but that spontaneity no longer existed between her and Geoff. It hadn't for ages, and why she let herself engage in such masochistic yearnings was beyond her.

"Hey, Marion!" Robyn hugged her warmly. "Come on and meet Nate's family."

Mrs. Lloyd was a pretty woman, short and pleasantly plump. "It's very nice to meet you." She smiled so hard her eyes were mere crescents. "Nate has talked so much about you."

Marion assiduously avoided Geoff's eyes.

"You've been wonderful to the kids," Mr. Lloyd said, pumping their hands in turn. "Having this wedding and all."

Nate's sister, Carol, a slim thirty-year-old, came forward carrying a toddler. Her husband, David, followed, leading a five-year-old boy by the hand.

For one unguarded moment Marion found herself gazing at the young family with longing. *This could've been me and Geoff,* she thought, *if things had worked out.*

"Hi. Oh, she's adorable." Marion admired the baby with what she hoped was just ordinary enthusiasm. "How old is she?"

Nate helped his grandmother out of the car, and soon all introductions were complete. The Lloyds were wonderful people, quite down-to-earth, and Marion liked them instinctively. But she sensed they were feeling a little shy so far from home.

She glanced at Geoff, silently imploring him to help ease their anxiety. She wasn't sure he understood. He would have once upon a time, but times had changed.

"I'm dying to see the yard, sis."

"And I'm dying to show it to you, but the tent crew's still here finishing up a few details. Why don't we go inside and relax awhile, wait till they're done?"

They moved inside to the living room, and Marion left them to prepare a tray of cold drinks in the kitchen.

When she returned, she found the room alive with activity and conversation. She paused in the doorway, amazed. She'd always depended on Geoff's personable nature in social situations, and he had come through again.

He had Mr. and Mrs. Lloyd and the grandmother poking into the ancient fireplace and chatting up a storm about flues. He'd directed Carol and Robyn to the mound of wedding gifts that had accumulated over the past week, and Nate and his brother-in-law were tumbling on the rug with the children.

The Lloyds were infatuated with the house, with the eighteenth-century details so lovingly preserved and the antiques Geoff and Marion had restored. She was showing them through the bedrooms when her parents arrived. She excused herself, leaving the tour to Geoff, and ran out to meet the car.

Marion hadn't seen her parents in five months, and when her mother hugged her, her emotions billowed.

"What's this, what's this?" Sara Chace laughed, smoothing back Marion's hair.

Marion smiled but her lips trembled. How she wished she had her parents closer now that she was pregnant and about to be single again.

"I think she's missed us, Henry. Oh, come here." Her mother embraced her again. "Why didn't you let us fly up sooner to help?"

"It wasn't necessary, Mom. Everything's under control."

"How've you been, pigtail?" Her father hugged her tight.

"Good, Dad." She blinked back tears.

"Well, you're looking more beautiful than ever."

"I think she looks thin, Henry," her mother contradicted.

"How's the store?" he asked, used to ignoring his wife's anxiety over their children.

"It's doing well. Want to stop by this week and make sure?"

His eyes lit up. "Do you mind?"

"Not at all. But now come inside and meet everybody. I think you and the Lloyds are going to hit it off."

They had lunch in the dining room, and while they ate, conversation flowed in half a dozen currents, sweetened by laughter and the piping chatter of children.

This is the way it used to be, Marion thought, remembering countless meals she and Geoff had shared at this table with family and friends. She glanced up from the lemon pie she was cutting and met Geoff's eyes. He was standing at the opposite end of the table pouring coffee. And that was how it used to be, too. Same places. Same tasks. She'd forgotten, but it was all coming back.

Passing each other in the kitchen doorway, his hand touched the same familiar place at her waist it had always touched. When she told an old anecdote, he jumped in with the expected lines.

Marion marveled at Geoff's acting ability. He'd assumed his role with astonishing authority. In fact, he was making it *too* real for her—the harmony, the conviviality, the sense of still being loved—and while that made it easier for her to behave in kind, the ache in her heart only continued to deepen. For as much as they seemed to be permanently woven into the grand scheme of things, the truth that they were not was never far beneath the surface of her smile.

Finally, with dishes cleared, Geoff suggested they all move outside to see the yard.

"Oh, I love it!" Robyn dashed into the tent. "It's wonderful! Nate, don't you love it?" She twirled between the tables.

"Wait till you see this." Geoff plugged two cords together and the inside of the tent came to twinkling life with thousands of tiny white lights. They were everywhere—around support poles, within potted trees, but especially overhead, forming a starry interior canopy.

Gazing upward, Robyn gasped. "Amazing. Absolutely amazing."

"Oh, Marion, this is spectacular." Her mother reached up to finger one of the dozens of silver and blue streamers glittering in the light breeze.

"Goodness, even a dance floor?" Carol exclaimed. Her children were already testing it.

Mr. Lloyd's eyes, meanwhile, were moving over the mountain of chairs, stacks of linens and the lumber Geoff and Marion had been hoping to transform into a platform for the band. "Looks like there's still a few chores left to do."

Marion sighed. She had been hoping to be further along by this time.

"Do you mind if we help?" he asked.

Marion began to protest, but Mrs. Lloyd joined her husband. "Oh, please. We'd feel so much more a part of this wedding if we could do something."

Marion and Geoff exchanged glances and shrugged.

"Sure," she answered. "But first you guys have to go pick up your tuxes."

By the time they were climbing into their cars to drive to rehearsal, everything that had needed doing was done. Even the luminarias edging the walks were in place. Tired but pleased, Marion sank into the soft leather seat of Geoff's car.

"How do you think we're doing?" he asked, driving along the country road to the Powell estate.

"For the most part, we deserve an A. We've been married so long I guess a lot of our behavior is second nature. Only my mother noticed something odd. She's always been too sharp for comfort. She asked if anything was bothering us."

"What did you say?"

"I blamed it on the wedding."

"I hope that satisfied her." Geoff drummed his wedding band on the wheel. "I've always had a soft spot for your mother."

"This is tougher than I thought, Geoff." Marion turned her troubled gaze out the side window, hoping he wouldn't ask her to explain. Hoping he thought she was upset merely by the prospect of hurting her family. Hoping he didn't guess the real difficulty lay in her coping with *him*.

"Try to relax," he offered. "You'll find it easier if you do." They'd reached the estate by then and the subject was dropped.

Geoff drove through the gate, making sure the other cars were right behind. Everyone who'd been at the house had come along since they'd be leaving directly after the rehearsal to go to dinner.

After passing the original Powell farmhouse and barn, the driveway curved gently to the left, rising all the while to the mansion and museum and the small stone chapel on the hill.

"Oh, this view is breathtaking." Standing outside the chapel, Mrs. Lloyd lay her dimpled hands on her chest and sighed.

"You can see right to the outer harbor from here," Geoff told her. "See?" He leaned close and pointed.

The woman smiled up at Geoff and practically twinkled. Looking on, Marion suppressed a smile. When Geoffrey Kent turned on the charm, no one was safe.

Mr. Lloyd, meanwhile, was studying the chapel. "My, this is different. Looks like something you'd find in a small English village."

"Close, Dad." Nate looked impressed. "If you had said Wales, you would've hit it right on the nose." Robyn looped two arms around his waist. "Well," he said, turning with her toward the side entrance, "we'd better get this over with."

"Are you sure you're not getting cold feet?" Robyn teased. "This time tomorrow..." She mimicked a noose being tightened around her neck.

Nate laughed and opened the heavy wooden door.

Geoff followed at the rear of the group. He paused at the door. "Coming, Marion?" His head tilted inquisitively.

Marion suddenly realized she hadn't said a word since getting out of the car and, in fact, was still leaning back on the fender, gazing at the chapel. Being here was having an effect on her she hadn't anticipated. Like lunch today, it was stirring up forgotten memories and unwanted feelings.

She cleared her throat with difficulty. "Yes. Wait up."

Inside, late-afternoon light poured through the diamond-shaped panes of the west-facing windows. The windows were high and narrow, only three on a side.

"Oh, it's..." Nate's sister hesitated, dismay in her eyes.

"Simple," Marion finished for her, smiling. "You might even call it stark."

"I'm sorry." Carol's color heightened. "I'm just accustomed to stained glass and lots of elaborate trimmings." Her eyes moved over the plain whitewashed walls to the place in front where she was probably used to seeing an altar. There she found nothing but an unadorned pulpit and a simple divided rail separating it from the general seating.

"Don't apologize. People are always surprised the first time they see this chapel. There's no organ, no choir loft, no bell to ring. They think, why would anyone ever want to be married here?"

"I...like it." Mrs. Lloyd smiled with growing conviction. "I really do. There's something...special here."

Mr. Lloyd nodded in agreement. "My Nate says you've all been married in this chapel. That right?"

Marion's father answered that yes, indeed, they had.

"Well, I hope this place blesses the kids the same as it's blessed you."

Marion glanced toward Geoff and wondered how he was able to keep up such a perfect front. "Geoff has ancestors who helped build the chapel," she cut in raggedly, hoping to divert the topic.

"That right?" Mr. Lloyd's eyes brightened.

"Not the structure," Geoff explained. "My people were carpenters. But knowing how uncomfortable these pews can get, I'm not sure I want to associate myself with them."

They were still laughing when the door opened.

"Hello-o," Bronwyn called cheerily. She propped open the door for air, then strode forward dressed in khaki bush shorts and a jungle-patterned shirt. Marion introduced her to the Lloyds, enjoying their surprise.

Mr. Lloyd chuckled. "You're not quite what I pictured when my Nate said he was going to be married by a justice of the peace."

"Don't worry, Mr. Lloyd. His marriage will be perfectly legal and binding. And, oh, yes, I'll try to find something else to wear."

They chatted awhile, but finally Bronwyn suggested they get started. First she explained to Nate's brother-in-law what was expected of him as an usher. She showed Nate and Geoff where to stand. Then she led Robyn, Marion and their father toward the back entrance.

Bronwyn had a pleasant way of keeping rehearsals lighthearted, knowing how tense things could get the night before a ceremony. Soon she had everyone laughing at her off-key rendition of "The Wedding March" and her exaggerated step-touch-step down the aisle.

Marion laughed along with the others, but the sense of déjà vu she'd begun to feel outside the chapel continued to rise within her, shaking her composure. She tried to ignore it, but it persisted, coming at her in the most insidious ways. In the angle of summer light that streamed through the windows. In the scent of furniture polish lifting off the slatted benches....

Soon the evening of her own wedding rehearsal melded so seamlessly with the present that Marion found herself not only remembering long-forgotten details—like the blue cotton shirt Geoff had been wearing—but she began to experience the same feelings she'd had that evening, too. The anticipation, the nervousness, the joy of knowing this would be the very last night she and Geoff would ever have to sleep apart.

The irony of the situation didn't escape her. They hadn't slept in the same bed for four weeks, and after tomorrow they wouldn't even share the same house.

When rehearsal ended—none too soon for Marion—everyone drove to the Haven Inn. But even there, memories hounded her. She and Geoff had come to this inn for their post-rehearsal dinner, too. She remembered who sat where, what she'd eaten, the three-piece band playing in the next room.

Under happier circumstances, she wouldn't have minded this deluge of memories. But tonight they seemed intent on underscoring how happy she and Geoff once had been—and how wretched they were now.

Mercifully everyone agreed they wanted to retire early, and Marion and Geoff were home by ten.

"Is there anything left to do?" he asked, turning off the car ignition.

"No. Just the dishes in the dishwasher. Oh, and my nails."

Geoff smiled softly. "You sound tired. Why not call it a night. Those things can get done in the morning."

Marion didn't expect him to reach across the darkness and touch her—a light stroking of his fingertips along her jaw. Neither did she expect to lean into that touch, as if inviting it to stay.

With a start, she pulled back. Dear Lord, what were they doing? No one else was here. Who were they performing for?

Eyes wild with confusion, she opened the car door and hurried toward the house. But even as she lay alone in their bed hours later, the impression of his fingers still burned along her cheek. She wondered, if this was just the rehearsal, how she was ever going to get through the real thing?

CHAPTER ELEVEN

STANDING INSIDE the covered entrance at the back of the chapel, Marion fluffed out Robyn's veil.

"Did it get very crushed on the ride over?" Robyn asked with concern in her big blue eyes.

"No, honey, it's fine. I'm just fussing."

Their mother was carefully spreading Robyn's train. Her gown was full-skirted and made of summer satin encrusted with thousands of seed pearls and aleçon lace. If Robyn had had months to choose it, Marion doubted she would've found a confection that made her look more like a princess.

Nearby, their father looked on wistfully, while from inside the chapel drifted the sweet strains of Liszt's "Lieberstraum."

"I still can't believe you got that string quartet." Robyn's eyes glistened. "You're too much, sis."

"Nothing to it. Especially with Mom and Dad footing the bill," Marion tried to joke to keep her emotions from rising too near the surface.

"Seriously, Marion, this is so much more than I expected. I don't know how to thank you."

"Just..." Marion had to pause to swallow back tears. "Just be happy."

Nate's brother-in-law leaned into the entry. "All set, Mrs. Chace?" Mr. and Mrs. Lloyd and Nate's grandmother had already been seated, and now the congregation was waiting eagerly for the mother of the bride.

Sara Chace's shoulders lifted with her quick indrawn breath. She nodded and then gave Robyn a hug. Her lower lip quivered as she whispered her blessings in her daughter's ear.

"Do I look all right, Marion?" she inquired, smoothing her pink tapestry jacket.

"Absolutely beautiful, Mom."

Her mother took the usher's arm and, raising her chin, walked into the chapel.

"Okay, Dad. Looks like we're on." Marion gestured for him to take Robyn's arm.

Henry Chace tugged at his tie and cleared his throat. Marion felt her eyes burn at seeing her father, this man who had always been a rock of emotional strength, having such difficulty keeping his composure.

The chapel was filled with family and friends, and when "The Wedding March" began, they got to their feet. Marion, however, was only vaguely aware of the curious faces ahead of her. She was too busy checking out the satin bows on the pews and the bouquets of flowers up front. Everything was in place and absolutely lovely. She smiled with relief and started down the aisle.

Bronwyn stood at the front of the congregation, dressed in a dark blue suit of raw linen. To the right stood a dashingly tuxedoed Nate, looking every inch the nervous but eager bridegroom. His eyes were trained on a point behind Marion.

Hesitantly Marion let her gaze move to Geoff, standing straight and tall at Nate's side. His eyes were fixed on her, just as Nate's were fixed on his bride. Suddenly Marion's heart was beating so wildly she was amazed she could still breathe. She tried looking away but was drawn back magnetically. *Look at something else,* she implored him with her eyes. But his gaze didn't waver for a second, his eyes burning into her like fiery beacons.

The morning had been chaotic, and although they'd posed together for innumerable pictures before he'd left the house to meet Nate, she hadn't really *looked* at him. She'd been too preoccupied with petty worries—if he had the rings and where the devil was the cake.

Ever careful to pace her steps with the music, she looked now, and her knees wobbled. Geoff was magnificent!

She reminded herself that this was the same man she'd slept with for thousands of nights, eaten meals with for thousands of days. He'd stopped being a surprise to her long ago. But nothing she said made any difference. At this moment, she felt as heady as any bride.

She was aware of his gaze moving over her. She was wearing a gown of palest blue, a shade that had always flattered her fair coloring, while the simple flowing design accentuated her curves. She'd gone to the beauty shop this morning and had her hair styled in an upswept 'do, curls cascading softly from the crown of her head around a spray of flowers pinned to one side. She felt fragile today, feminine, and when she saw the admiration in Geoff's eyes, she also began to feel pretty.

Oh, she had to get a grip on herself, and soon. This make-believe was becoming too real. If she didn't she was going to make a fool of herself before the day was over.

At the front of the chapel she stepped to the left, making way for her father and Robyn. She half turned so that she and Geoff were facing each other. Her stomach fluttered crazily.

Bronwyn asked, "Who represents the families in blessing this marriage?"

"I do," her father answered. He kissed Robyn's cheek and went to join his wife in the front pew while Nate stepped to Robyn's side.

Marion swallowed repeatedly, trying to ease the lump in her throat. Six feet away, Geoff smiled softly, as if he understood the difficulty she was having seeing her little sister get married.

"Marion?" Bronwyn's eyes darted to the chairs in front of the rail.

Marion lifted one of them, set it behind Robyn and helped her sit. Likewise, Geoff provided a chair for Nate. Then he and Marion sat down, too.

"Please be seated, everyone," Bronwyn invited.

Marion knew Bronwyn intended to say a few words before the ceremony. She'd mentioned it at rehearsal. But Marion had no idea what message those words would impart.

"Good afternoon," Bronwyn said, smiling over the settling congregation. "We're gathered here today to witness the joining of two of the nicest people I've ever had the privilege of knowing. Nate. Robyn." Her smile warmed as she looked down at them. Marion saw Nate reach for Robyn's hand.

"For those of you who may not be familiar with the Eternity Chapel and are wondering why this otherwise sane and considerate couple coerced their families into pulling together a wedding on three weeks' notice just so they could be married here—" the chapel rustled with laughter "—I'd like to tell you a little about the place."

Marion stopped breathing. Bronwyn was going to talk about the legend, that dumb childish legend. She'd bet money on it.

"There's a legend associated with this chapel..."

Marion slid down in her seat. Although she and Bronwyn had spoken several times since meeting outside the market, they'd never again discussed the legend. Their ideas were too disparate, and the subject remained a silent breach between them.

"...a legend that claims no marriage solemnized here will ever end unhappily. As a result, couples have been coming to this chapel to be married for more than a century now, never questioning whether that legend had any truth to it. Until recently, I shared the same unquestioning faith.

"But a few weeks ago, someone said to me, 'Bronwyn, think a minute. Considering the staggering numbers of people who've been married here, do you really believe that not one of those couples has divorced or had an unhappy marriage?' "

Marion slid down another inch in her seat. From the corner of her eye she saw Geoff looking at her, one eyebrow cocked.

"Needless to say, that person's comment bothered me tremendously. But it also got me thinking. Eventually I arrived at a few ideas I'd like to share with you today, Robyn and Nate. I hope they'll be of some value in the future." Bronwyn paused. The chapel was so quiet Marion could hear birds chirping outside.

"Too often, people think that being married in this chapel is an easy guarantee they won't have problems. But life is full of problems, and all couples are tested, no matter who they are or where they were married. This chapel doesn't place a magic protective shell around anyone."

Bronwyn continued to address Robyn and Nate, but Marion's skin prickled with the suspicion that her words were meant for her and Geoff.

"In this regard," Bronwyn went on, "I agree with my skeptical friend, and to be perfectly honest, I really don't understand the legend myself. Statistics clearly prove that marriage is a dicey business these days. One in every two ends in divorce. So, taking numbers and probability into account, the legend *doesn't* make rational sense, does it?

"Yet I've never heard of a couple breaking up after being married here, so I can only assume that chapel couples really do have something going for them." Bronwyn scanned her attentive audience.

"And this is what I think it is. Couples married here all believe in the possibility of a happy marriage. More importantly, they all expect to enjoy one. Consequently, when the bad times come, they work through them somehow, because the prospect of not doing so simply doesn't exist for them. In other words, the legend becomes a self-fulfilling prophecy, the magic lying not in the chapel itself, but within the people married here." Her eyes flicked briefly to Marion and Geoff.

Marion's fingers tightened around her bouquet. Geoff folded his arms.

"Right now, Robyn and Nate, you're enjoying a stage in your lives so intensely blissful you probably aren't even listening to these words about bad times. But, sorry to say, that honeymoon stage will pass. It's only natural. And when it does, you might find your marriage in its first crisis. If you're like some couples, you might start thinking the magic has gone out of your relationship."

Marion kept her eyes on her flowers. Not a doubt remained who the real target of this talk was.

"But I'd like to propose that the magic hasn't died. The relationship has merely entered a time of change, change that should be expected and must be embraced if a marriage is to last. Because marriage does not stand still. It flows. Like the river running through this town, it flows and changes and becomes something new at each bend and strait.

"At one time, career conflicts may cause you marital friction. At another time, it might be the demands of raising children. Marriage flows, on to the time of the empty nest, on to retirement, and at each juncture you may find your relationship being challenged and redefined.

"It can be a hair-raising journey—or it can be a wonderful and exciting one. The trick is, you've got to remember not to let go of each other as you take the ride. Let go, and you just might drift apart. Remember to keep talking. Don't be afraid to share your fears and your needs. Compromise and, above all, listen. The power to keep your marriage alive and vibrant is in your hands."

Marion pressed her fingertips to her forehead and under the cover of her hand glanced at Geoff. He was looking back.

"You're probably wondering where I'm going with this advice and if I'll ever get back to the chapel. Well, yes, and here's my point. It's easy for couples to believe in legends when they're young. All of life's possibilities are just opening up to them. It's later, when things haven't turned out quite as we expected, that believing becomes difficult. But that's when we need our legends most, because they contain our most cherished beliefs and ideals. And maybe therein lies the true secret of this chapel, in a couple's willingness to believe that when the magic dies—" Marion felt

Bronwyn's gaze on her lowered head "—you cast another spell."

In the deep silence that followed, someone at the back of the chapel coughed. It sounded like an explosion.

Bronwyn went on to extend her best wishes to the young couple and then said, "Nate and Robyn, will you stand, please?"

They did, and Marion and Geoff removed the chairs and stood with them. Marion's legs quivered. Bronwyn had meant to lecture them, and Marion indeed felt chastised.

Bronwyn opened her black leather book and asked the couple to join hands and repeat after her.

"I, Nathan Thomas Lloyd..."

Marion heard the words of the familiar vows as in a dream. They swirled in her mind, mingling with words from the past. *I, Geoffrey Michael Kent...*

"Take thee, Robyn Marie Chace..."

Take thee, Marion Brett Chace...

Timidly she gazed across the aisle. Geoff was watching her, a bright intentness in his dark eyes. *What are you thinking, Geoff?*

"For better or for worse..."

Is there the wildest chance that you're thinking we gave up too easily?

"For richer or for poorer..."

The remotest possibility that you think we can still work through our differences?

"In sickness and in health..."

Or am I just succumbing to the romance of this wedding, letting sentimentality get the better of me?

Bronwyn called for the rings, and Marion watched Geoff hand them over.

"With this ring..." Robyn was murmuring.

Marion gazed at Geoff's hands, clasped loosely in front of him, at the wedding band he still wore. She'd engraved, "For always," inside his ring; "And forever," inside hers.

She chided herself for dwelling on such things. Nostalgia would only make the day impossible to endure.

But her heart went on aching, anyway. For as much as she'd loved her husband when she'd slipped that ring on his finger, she loved him even more now, far, far more.

"By the power vested in me by the commonwealth of Massachusetts..."

Marion was jarred by the realization that the service was ending.

"I now pronounce you husband and wife."

Nate and Robyn kissed, and the sounds of clapping and happy murmurs lifted from the congregation, while the musicians struck up a sweetly triumphant recesssional.

Marion leaned toward Bronwyn, not quite meeting her eyes. "It was a lovely service."

"Well, I gave it my best shot." She looked from Marion to Geoff with concern.

"You have one more wedding, right?"

"Right, but I'll see you as soon as that's done." She squeezed Marion's arm and motioned her toward Geoff, who was waiting to escort her up the aisle.

Marion turned slowly, her breathing stalled. Under Geoff's bright searching eyes, she felt shy and uncertain. His strong beautifully shaped lips twisted into a small assured smile. He offered her his arm, and with a strange quiver of excitement shooting through her, she took it.

THEY WERE THE FIRST to arrive at the house, and as soon as the car came to a stop in the driveway, Marion dashed into the yard to make sure everything was in order. Graham had skipped the chapel service to oversee last-minute preparations. Walking toward the tent, she now had to admit everything looked fabulous.

The interior was a sea of soft blue, accented with cream and navy—the effect created by crisp table linens and a profusion of flowers. Crystal sparkled everywhere.

The long buffet table stood at the end of the tent nearest the house, gleaming with ornate chafing dishes and silver urns. At the opposite end stretched the elegant head table with two large candelabra and magnificent sprays of flowers that ran the table's entire length.

To one side, on its own lace-covered table, stood the cake. Marion's heart rate calmed measurably. When they'd left for the chapel, the cake hadn't yet arrived. To the other side, the band Honeymooners that Bronwyn had miraculously procured was conducting a last-minute sound check. Its vocalist, Kerry Muldoon, waved at Marion from behind the microphone, assuring her that everything was fine. In the center of the tent lay the wooden dance floor, with the dining tables arranged all around.

Marion felt a hand at her waist, a hand whose size and shape she knew instinctively. She tried to block it out. She didn't want to feel anything this close to his leaving. But she failed miserably.

"Guests are arriving. Robyn wants us in the receiving line." Geoff turned her to face him, keeping his hands at her waist.

Slowly Marion looked up, bracing herself for the effect he was having on her today. For whatever reason, alone or with an audience, he just wasn't turning off the charm.

"You have rose petals caught in your hair," he said.

"Oh." Dismayed, she lifted one hand.

"Wait. I'll get them." Geoff picked carefully between her curls. He was standing so close his breath fanned her cheek.

Marion stood very still, trying to conceal that his gentle touch was sending shivers throughout her body.

When she peeked up at him, however, the confident gleam in his eyes told her she wasn't concealing much.

"There, I think I got most of them."

"Thank you."

His grin broadened as his gaze swept downward over her gown and back up to her eyes. "My pleasure. Come on, we shouldn't keep our guests waiting."

The reception flowed smoothly, much to Marion's relief. Guests mingled for a leisurely hour on the lawn, sipping champagne and having their pictures taken, while the musicians played soft jazz in the background.

As hosts, Marion and Geoff mingled, too, but with frequent trips to the kitchen to check on the caterers. They weren't really able to relax until dinner.

They sat at the head table, Marion to the side of the groom, Geoff to the side of the bride. While waiters served their table, guests helped themselves to a sumptuous buffet that included a rich lobster casserole, a whole side of beef, ham, chicken and several kinds of salads and vegetables.

Marion's parents sat to her other side, and while she ate she chatted with them or with Nate. Yet throughout, her mind was preoccupied with an awareness of Geoff. Over the buzz of conversation, she easily discerned his deep voice. Across the laden plates, she recognized his hands shifting utensils, reaching for wine—movements she'd watched a million times yet today found totally novel and compelling.

Occasionally he tipped his chair back and caught her eye, just long enough to wink or give her a quick admiring once-over. Marion told herself to ignore him. His flirtatious behavior was all just part of the charade. But an excitement was building in her blood she couldn't ignore, a sense of something wonderful about to unfold. And it wasn't fair. She wished he'd stop.

The meal was interrupted continuously by the insistent tinging of spoons against wineglasses, calling for the bride and groom to kiss. And they did, every time, without hesitation.

Marion tried to ignore that, too. After the eighth kiss, she turned to her parents and engaged them in conversation for the rest of the meal.

Her parents were in high spirits now that the ceremony was over, and before long Marion was feeling not only calmer but almost festive. Although she'd decided not to drink while she was pregnant, she allowed herself a small glass of wine.

By the time Robyn and Nate got up to cut the cake, Marion's head felt light, and turning to Geoff, she wore an unabashed smile. With the chairs between them unoccupied, they were finally able to see each other unimpeded.

"I swear, if Robyn smooshes cake in Nate's face," she said, "I'll choke her."

Geoff leaned toward her, his arm extended over the backs of the empty chairs, his fingertips just touching her shoulder. "How many of these corny rituals are we going to have to put up with today?" His eyes glittered, his strong lips curved in a tantalizing half smile. Off to the side, the newlyweds were slicing into the three-tiered cake, larger hand over smaller hand, while Kerry sang, "The bride cuts the cake..."

"Just about all of them," Marion answered.

"Ah, well, it looks like it's going to be a good party, anyway."

"Yes. There are lots of young people here to keep it lively."

"We're not exactly old, Marion."

Sudden laughter drew Marion's gaze away. "Oh, no, she did it!"

Geoff sat back. "Get used to it, Nate," he called out.

Nate wiped the frosting off his cheek, and then it was Robyn's turn. But he merely held the cake to his bride's lips and let her take a delicate bite. A communal "aw" applauded his thoughtfulness, and while Robyn was still chewing, he drew her to him and kissed her.

"My sister blushing?" Marion said, delighted. "This is a first."

Geoff and Marion turned to each other, smiling freely and naturally, and she realized it had been a very long time since they'd done that, smiled directly at each other and *with* each other.

Their smiles faded, but they continued to stare. Marion's heart thumped harder with each passing second. *It's just pretend,* she told herself repeatedly. *Geoff doesn't really mean this.*

But the attraction pulsing between them refused to subside. If anything, it deepened, and Marion began to think that what was happening was very real indeed. Only when

Robyn and Nate returned to their seats did she feel released.

As soon as the meal ended, Marion left her seat.

Geoff called after her. "What are you doing?"

Escaping, she thought. *Running off to catch my breath.* "I haven't said hello to my uncle Stuart yet." And before Geoff could offer to join her, she dashed off.

Everyone was getting up now, and from the corner of her eye she noticed Geoff do the same. She watched to see if he'd follow her. He didn't. He crossed the dance floor and clapped Graham on the back.

Marion had seated Graham with two attractive single women, and now he was introducing them to Geoff. Marion continued her conversation with her uncle, but her eyes kept flicking aside, taking in the women's overt flirtations.

Just when she thought her teeth might crack from grinding them so hard, Geoff moved on.

They continued to mill, taking separate paths, yet Marion never once lost awareness of where Geoff was. His dark good looks and tall commanding presence drew her like a magnet. She could turn and find him instantly, and as often as she did, she found him looking back. This visual pursuit unnerved her and thrilled her and more than anything confused her.

She was just saying hello to Bronwyn when Kerry took the microphone and called for Nate and Robyn to step out onto the dance floor for their first dance. Then the musicians eased into a lovely rendition of "Unchained Melody."

Marion's eyes filled, watching Robyn and Nate embrace. Her little sister was all grown-up and about to go far away and be a wife.

Though her vision was swimming, Marion noticed Geoff studying her from across the dance floor. Her breath came up short. Would they be expected to dance, as well?

Kerry called for the parents of the bride and groom, and they, too, stepped on to the floor. Marion looked away from Geoff, trying to appear composed, but her heart was slamming like a jackhammer. *Marion, get hold of yourself. You've danced with the man a thousand times.*

But the slate of time had been wiped clean, and for all her heart knew this could be their very first dance.

Finally it came, the call for the best man and matron of honor. Keeping to the edges of the floor, Geoff strode toward her in an unhurried loose-limbed gait. Still she felt rushed. Her mouth was dry, her thoughts spinning.

"We haven't d-danced in so long," she stammered, staring at his proffered hand. "I'm not sure I remember how."

"Like riding a bicycle," he murmured. "It'll come back."

Marion fit her hand in his, walked out to the middle of the floor and let him turn her in his arms. She hoped he didn't feel the tremor that racked her when his palm touched her back.

"Robyn looks happy," she said more to fill the silence between them than anything else.

"Nate, too. They're going to be good together."

"I hope." She tried to laugh. "Do you realize we're their role models, Geoff?"

He fixed his gaze over her head and after a moment said the most remarkable thing. "Well, what's wrong with that?"

Before Marion could shake off her astonishment, someone cut in. Everyone was changing partners, and with a disappointed sigh she watched her mother make off with Geoff. Her disappointment deepened when she realized that she and her husband had probably just done all the dancing they were going to do at this wedding.

Well, it was probably for the best. Dancing with Geoff, not dancing with Geoff—what did it matter on the eve of his leaving? All it was doing was driving her crazy, anyway.

Marion finished out the dance with her father, and then hurried to the house where she was kept busy for the next hour helping the caterers, making sure the bar stayed stocked and everyone got their cake. Small emergencies arose—a bandage was needed for a child's scraped knee, aspirins for an aunt's headache. She didn't mind; this was her role today, she told herself, listening to the laughter and music through the kitchen window. The reception seemed to be shifting gear as shadows lengthened, quickly losing its formality and becoming a genuine party. She'd glanced out the window often enough to know Geoff was right in the swing of things, too.

"Marion, we need you out here," Bronwyn called through the screen door.

"What? Is the coffee urn empty again?" Marion came out to the porch wiping her hands on her apron.

"No, it isn't the coffee urn." Bronwyn chuckled.

Standing at the microphone, Kerry addressed her. "Come down here, Marion."

She shot Bronwyn an alarmed look. "What's going on?"

"Go," her friend urged.

Marion took off her apron, hooked it on the porch rail and entered the tent. The dance floor was cleared, and everyone was looking at her. She found Geoff standing a short distance away, and when her eyes questioned his, he shrugged.

"Marion. Geoff. Word has just reached this stage that you two will be celebrating an anniversary next week."

Marion's stomach fluttered up to her mouth. Across the way Geoff pulled in a sudden breath. He swung toward Graham. "You!" he accused good-naturedly. Everyone was laughing, enjoying this new turn in the day's entertainment.

"Come up here, you two," Kerry coaxed.

Smiling on the outside but trembling within, Marion met Geoff in front of the band's raised platform.

"Just to exonerate Dr. Reed," the singer continued, "he isn't the only person who squealed. You've got more enemies at this bash than you realize." Everyone laughed again.

"But since he was best man at your wedding, he's asked if he could do the honors."

While Graham walked to the stage, Marion glanced up at Geoff. "Are you sure you weren't in on this?"

Geoff shook his head. "I swear to you—"

"Honestly, between him and Bronwyn... We need some new friends, Geoffrey."

"You're right. If he dares say anything embarrassing—"

By then Graham had adjusted the mike. "Will everyone raise their glasses with me, please?"

Marion's mother hurried over with two glasses and handed them to Geoff and Marion.

"Marion, Geoff," Graham intoned solemnly, then he paused and laughed. "Boy, I wish you two could see how scared you look. I'm gonna be good, honestly." He cleared his throat, composing himself. "Marion, Geoff," he began again, "I'm not exactly the most romantic guy in the world, and I don't usually subscribe to the old one-and-only philosophy of love, but when I look at you two, you make me a believer. For eleven years you've shown us all how great married life can be, and today we want to thank you for having the good sense to find each other and make it a permanent thing." He raised his glass. "Congratulations, my friends, and continued health, happiness and a lifetime of love."

A chorus of "Hear, hear" lifted from the surrounding crowd.

"Marion?"

"Oh." She gave a start, realizing Geoff was waiting, glass raised. She touched her glass to his, meeting his eyes fleetingly and took a sip. Immediately he removed the glass from her hand, set it on a nearby table and led her by the hand to the center of the floor, while the band slid into the introductory bars of a slow number.

Kerry again took the mike while Graham returned to the sidelines. "This is an old tune, ladies and gentlemen, one of those dreamy romantic ones from the forties. It's called 'There Will Never Be Another You.'"

Marion gulped. "This isn't fair," she said in an undertone.

"In love and war, all's fair," Geoff said, turning to her and raising his arms in invitation. "Come here, Mrs. Kent."

Marion wasn't sure where she got the strength to move. She felt boneless, nerveless, breathless, as she gazed into her husband's dark burning eyes. Trancelike, she stepped into his embrace and trembled as his arms enfolded her. Somewhere on the edges of her awareness she heard applause. For them? What for? They'd failed. They were splitting up.

But it was hard to remember their failure when Geoff was holding her so close. Hard to imagine him driving away when their hearts were drumming in time.

Kerry began to sing in her clear strong voice, and before long Marion wasn't even aware of where they were. Their surroundings faded, leaving them at a place where only they and the romantic music existed.

Geoff pulled Marion closer and whispered, "Are you okay?"

"No," she complained dreamily into the warm crook of his neck. "I think I'm going to faint."

"Don't worry. I'll hold you up, keep moving you around the floor. You know, like a big old mop. No one'll notice."

Marion laughed softly and felt Geoff smiling against her ear. From the sidelines, laughter.

"Geoff, everybody's watching us."

"Would you prefer they turned their backs? This *is* our dance."

She sighed, melting into him. "Yes, it is." And it might also be the last dance they ever shared. Suddenly Marion wanted to make the most of it. She closed her eyes and wound both her arms around his neck. She wasn't going to fight her feelings anymore. Just for a few minutes she was going to surrender, soak up his heat and strength, let her senses revel in his fragrance, in his hardness, in the reassuring beat of his pulse....

Fleetingly an image of Tiffany flashed across Marion's mind, but Geoff pressed her closer, his palms moving over her back in slow sensuous circles, and the image dissolved. His hips had come to fit with hers and now he and Marion were moving as one, breathing as one, to the slow tender rhythm.

Vaguely Marion thought she heard the singer chuckling and saying something like, "Are you taking notes, kids?" She didn't have the blurriest idea what Kerry meant.

All too soon the music ended, but for several precious moments Geoff and Marion remained clinging. She didn't want to move, but eventually Geoff eased his hold and she stepped back. She was surprised to see moisture clinging to his long eyelashes.

"Marion and Geoff Kent, ladies and gentlemen," Kerry announced in a congratulatory voice. Applause again, seeping through the golden haze that surrounded Marion as she watched Geoff watching her.

Would he kiss her? She sensed he was thinking about it.

But almost immediately a fast number began and other dancers moved onto the floor, breaking the spell. Marion stepped farther from her husband, clearing her throat, looking toward the house, wondering what she could possibly do to escape the heartache she was feeling now.

"Well, I'd better get back...."

Geoff suddenly gripped her wrist and pulled her to him so forcefully she crashed into his chest. Devilment glittered in his eyes as his arm slid around her waist. "Not so fast, Mrs. Kent," he murmured. Holding her firmly with one hand, he undid his tie with the other and, with the most irresistible of grins, said, "Let's dance."

CHAPTER TWELVE

EVENING DEEPENED to dusk, and the tiny lights crowding the tent's interior came to twinkling life. With the cooling shadows of encroaching night, the party heated up. The band was remarkably versatile, moving easily from "The Tennessee Waltz" to "The Electric Slide." Shoes got kicked off and jackets discarded. Children, like wood sprites, retreated to the denser darknesses where fireflies flickered.

"But I've never done the Achy Breaky," Marion wailed, her cheeks aglow. She and Geoff had been dancing all evening, leaving the floor only to get an occasional drink.

"You think I have?" Geoff tugged her into the dance line. "Let's go, lady. I refuse to make a fool of myself alone."

They were laughing so hard by the end of that number, her sides literally ached.

Dusk deepened into night, and they continued to dance, changing partners once in a while, but always coming back to each other.

"That man of yours has some pretty slick moves, sis," Robyn commented, pressing an ice cube to her flushed cheek. Marion forgot her intended lecture about how brides in full regalia did not do the chicken dance. It was Robyn's party and she could do as she pleased.

"He's wearing me out. Uh-oh. Here he comes again," Marion complained, even as her heart soared.

They danced fast, they danced slow, and as they danced, it occurred to Marion that sometime during the day she and Geoff had stopped pretending to have fun and the genuine thing had taken over. No longer a charade, their joy had become real.

She was at a loss as to how it had happened. Dancing? Was that what had finally got them to relax? At the same time she was reminded of all the other activities they used to enjoy together—hiking, hunting for antiques, playing cards, skiing, having friends over. But they'd stopped. Caught up in their separate lives, it had been ages since they'd *played* together, and now she could only wonder where their marriage would be if they'd made the time.

Finally she and Geoff collapsed on the back porch steps to sit out the throwing of the bouquet. The party was definitely winding down. A few people had already left. Two children were asleep on a quilt.

Floating in her own private euphoria, Marion sat one step below Geoff, resting back between his knees, his enveloping arms crossed possessively in front of her. When he spoke, his lips touched her ear. When he laughed, the sound rumbled through her.

Marion noticed Bronwyn watching them, smirking, as she stood with the other unmarried women, waiting for the bouquet toss. "I told you," she mouthed clearly enough for Marion to lip-read. A short distance away, Graham was wearing a similarly smug expression.

Even this morning Marion would have refuted them, but now all she could do was shrug sheepishly. Sitting here with Geoff felt too right, too much like where she belonged.

A drumroll sounded, and Robyn tossed her bouquet. One of her co-workers bounded into the air and caught the flowers in a pincer-tight grip. Now it was Bronwyn's turn to shrug. Marion laughed, resting her weight against Geoff. Bronwyn certainly hadn't tried very hard to become the next bride.

Marion let her contented gaze drift over the scene—all the people she loved most in the world were here. And there were so many. Her heart filled to overflowing.

She recalled telling Bronwyn that she and Geoff had nothing left in common. How wrong she'd been. They shared so much—a large loving family, this beautiful home, good friends, collective memories and a past full of passion and true caring.

And maybe...maybe they had a future, too, if they worked at it.

Robyn and Nate changed into their going-away clothes and then danced their last dance to "That's What Friends Are For," which reduced the women to tears and the men to striking overly nonchalant poses.

"Be happy for us, sis," Robyn said, hugging Marion.

"I am. Really I am," she replied, sobbing helplessly.

Robyn tried to tease. "Geoffrey, do something with your wife." But tears were trickling down her cheeks, too.

Half an hour later, everyone was gone—the guests, the family, even the band. Fingers entwined, Marion and Geoff strolled into the tent. She gazed up at the starry lights twinkling over-head, at the silver streamers turning slowly in the night air. Crickets provided the only music.

"Well, Geoffrey, we pulled it off," she said, turning to face him on the confetti-strewn dance floor.

"Yes. It was a beautiful wedding. Robyn and Nate will look back on this day with nothing but pleasant memories." But his smile faded, telling Marion he was aware they'd done more than that. They'd pulled off their ruse, convinced everyone they were still a happily married couple. It had been so easy, too. That's what amazed her. What had started as a difficult charade three weeks ago had today turned quite real.

"Thank you, Geoff."

"Please don't thank me. That makes it sound as if I was forced to do something I didn't want." He moved closer and clasped his hands loosely behind her back.

"When's the tent leaving?" he asked.

"Monday."

"Oh, good. Let's have everyone back for a barbecue tomorrow."

Marion laughed softly. She spread her hands on his shirtfront, feeling his warmth through the tucked material, reveling in the easy intimacy that they'd attained today and that persisted even now. It almost seemed, well, miraculous.

"Know what I enjoyed most?" His voice was dangerously soft as he pulled her closer. When their bodies met, Marion's eyes shut on an intake of breath.

"What?" she somehow replied while he continued to fit himself to her and she continued to melt.

His eyes smoldered under languorous half-closed lids. "Dancing with you again. It's been too long." His hands pressed down her back slowly, fingers spread as if seeking as much of her as possible.

"Mm. It was nice," she agreed, swaying with him ever so slightly to phantom music. Totally beguiled, she watched Geoff's face. The galaxy of overhead lights was throwing spangles over his cheekbones and thick dark hair. Over hers, too? she wondered. Where they caught in a cloud of magic dust?

"You were the most beautiful woman here. Did I tell you that?"

"Oh, stop." She smiled, snuggling into him to hide the color blooming in her cheeks.

"But you were," he insisted softly.

Her fingers twined in the long hair that curled over his collar. "The bride is always the most beautiful."

"Don't get me wrong." His parted lips feathered the side of her cheek, sending tremors through every part of her. "Robyn looked great, too. But she couldn't hold a candle to her big sister."

"Geoffrey, are you trying to seduce me?"

He laughed, a devilish rumble deep in his throat. "How am I doing?"

Marion lifted her head and on a terrifying leap of trust let him see—all the longing, all the love, shining in her eyes.

She felt the change that flowed physically through him. His body became taut, and the playfulness left his eyes to be replaced by unmitigated desire. And her whole being sang, *Yes! Oh, yes! Thank God and heaven, yes!* The next moment he was kissing her with an ardor that liquefied her bones.

They were both breathing raggedly when he finally lifted his head. "Oh, lady, you taste so good."

Rockets were still exploding all over her, inside, outside. "Then kiss me again," she said in a voice too husky to be her own.

He did. It was a kiss of pure possession that left no doubt where he wanted to lead her. She opened her mouth to him, answering that she wanted to follow. Immediately heat spilled through them both.

On an abrupt surge of need, Geoff swept Marion off her feet and into his arms, and strode determinedly toward the house. On the way, the flowers dropped from her hair to the star-dusted dance floor—and neither of them thought to turn off the lights.

Geoff nudged open the door of their bedroom and swung Marion inside. Her head reeled, partly from being carried, mostly from love for this man.

Beside the bed he set her on her feet, letting her body slide down his, slowly, provocatively. Holding her by the shoulders, he brushed his parted lips over hers, then rained a debilitating shower of soft kisses down her neck to the shadow between her breasts. Her skin, sensitized beyond anything she had ever known, seemed to catch fire.

She ran the tip of her tongue over her moist lips and tasted salt. His? she wondered. Or her own? She let her head fall back, glorying in the commingling, while the heat of his mouth spread through the fabric of her gown.

The room swam in watery light from the yard, enough light to see by as Geoff stepped back to unbutton his shirt, his strong fingers moving with grace and yet astonishing speed, his mesmerizing eyes never breaking their lock on hers.

Marion spread his shirt open and let her hands explore. His skin was warm, smooth over the shoulder, his chest all hard muscle and springy hair. Under her questing touch, Geoff closed his eyes and swallowed.

"I've missed you, Geoff," she whispered fervently.

"Oh, Marion, I've missed you." He spoke with an earnestness that bordered on desperation. Pulling her into his arms again, he covered her mouth with his. Her body felt fevered, pulsing everywhere, aching for him.

On the fuzzy edges of her consciousness, she heard the zipper at the back of her gown open with a long slow sigh. Gentle fingers, callused from yard work, slid under the silky material and slipped it off her shoulders. The next moment the garment lay in a puddle around her ankles. She stepped out of it and nudged it aside.

Two steps to the right, and they were sitting on the bed. Seconds later, they were lying down. And all the while they continued to kiss, exploring each other with a hunger born of weeks of separation.

With an expertise that came of eleven years' practice, Geoff removed her slip and sent it sliding to the floor. His trousers followed. Soon not a single barrier lay between them.

Looking up into Geoff's impossibly handsome face, Marion noticed a muscle twitch at the corner of his mouth.

"What are you smiling at?" she whispered, her hand cupping his jaw.

His smile broadened. "When we got married, we thought we knew it all." His emboldened gaze moved from her lips to her taut breasts. "Why didn't anybody tell us?"

"Tell us what?"

"How unbelievably good loving gets with time."

Marion breathed out a laugh, agreeing. "Geoff, I have so much to say..."

"I know. I do, too. But right now..." He shifted his weight so that his long virile body was pressing down on hers. "Right now I have a few other things on my mind," he whispered. He lowered his head and began to trace her smile with the tip of his tongue, and then to explore deeper, sending wave upon wave of heat crashing through her. Before long, their passion had reached so intense a pitch that all the words she wanted to say burned away to nothing. All except the silent prayer: *Please let me be enough.*

GEOFF WOKE SLOWLY—a euphoric floating sensation—and then he remembered why he felt so good this morning. He turned his head and gazed at his wife, still asleep, her lips parted slightly, blond curls tumbling everywhere. He smiled contentedly. Lord, you'd think they were the ones who'd gotten married yesterday, the way they'd made love last night.

He braced himself on his elbows and surveyed the room. Clothing was strewn everywhere. His smile deepened. He sat up carefully, eased himself off the mattress and quietly began to tidy the room.

He had Marion's gown hung, her shoes laid side by side and his tuxedo folded over a chair when he picked up her slip. Unthinkingly he opened her lingerie drawer to tuck the garment inside—and then realized she'd probably want to wash it before putting it away.

He was about to close the drawer when he saw the prescription bottle. He paused, frowning, and slowly picked it up. Was Marion sick?

He read the label, alarm making his mind a blank for several long seconds—right before his heart soared. Marion was pregnant?

He swung around, ready to wake her, ready to shout hallelujah to the rafters—when all at once his spirits crashed. Why hadn't she told him?

A calendar of appointments with Dr. Toomey also lay nestled in the drawer. Geoff scanned it, his fevered brain calculating quickly that she was already two months along. Two months!

He sank to a chair, feeling deprived of something vital. She'd learned she was pregnant and chose not to tell him, and a moment had passed that would never come again. Why? Why hadn't they celebrated? Why hadn't she shared this with him? Made plans? All that joy—withheld from him. Why?

An emptiness opened up inside him, a loneliness he'd hoped he'd never know again. He stared at his slumbering wife and felt like a stranger to her, someone looking in on her life from outside.

It hit him all at once, and the pain cut so hard that sweat beaded on his brow. Marion hadn't told him, because she didn't *want* him to know about the pregnancy. She'd planned to walk out of their marriage without ever telling him.

For the past couple of days he'd been deluding himself, thinking that Tiffany was the cause of their marital strife. But whether Tiffany had interfered or not didn't matter. Their lives had begun to change long before Tiffany came on the scene, but he'd locked onto Tiffany because she made an easy excuse, one he thought he had a chance of fighting.

Wishful thinking on his part. His and Marion's troubles ran a whole lot deeper than that. His first instinct had been right: he *had* become unnecessary in her life. So unnecessary she apparently didn't think she even needed him around to be a father to their child.

And then the pain cut still deeper. *That* was why she was in such a hurry to get him out of the house, why she'd overblown the kiss with Tiffany, why she'd leapt on the chance he might move to California to bring up the subject of divorce. She wanted him gone before her pregnancy began to show.

Geoff replaced the calendar and quietly closed the drawer. Then he slipped from the room and went down the hall to dress and think about what he was going to do with the rest of his life.

MARION PULLED on a pair of worn denim jeans and a white cotton T-shirt, ran a brush through her hair and raced down the stairs, jumping the last two steps.

"Geoff?" she called, poking her head into his study. Finding the room empty, she danced down the hall to the kitchen.

Coffee was made. She lifted the glass pot from its warming pad and, raising it to her nose, took a deep satisfying sniff. Had coffee ever smelled this good?

But she set the pot down, wanting Geoff more than coffee. Besides, she thought, placing two cradling hands over her stomach, the baby didn't need the caffeine.

She found him outside, sitting on the top step of the kitchen porch. He didn't turn when she opened the door.

"Good morning," she said brightly. He didn't answer. His shoulders were tensed and set high. His elbows rested on his knees, his linked hands pressed to his taut mouth. She stepped closer, frowning, a feeling of uneasiness creeping over her skin. This wasn't the mood she expected to find him in today.

And then it hit her—Geoff was still planning to leave. Nothing had changed. He'd been planning to leave even last night. He just didn't know how to tell her now, after making love. She clutched the porch rail to steady herself.

Oh, Lord, what had she done? Reality washed through her in a chilling tide as thoughts of Geoff's involvement with Tiffany arose, tangling with reminders of the opportunities Seatham was offering him.

Swept off her feet by the romance of being in her husband's arms again, she'd turned a blind eye to the fact that Tiffany and Seatham still existed. She'd let herself believe the charade was real and Geoff had decided to stay.

What a fool she was! Had he said anything about staying?

Summoning all the courage she had, she swallowed her tears and asked, "Do you want to talk about it?"

He turned, and that was when she saw the anguish in his eyes. "Yes, I think it's overdue." He hauled himself off the porch step. "Do you want to walk?"

With a feeling of blackest dread, she descended the steps where they'd sat last night, skirted the tent where they'd danced and slowly crossed the dewy lawn by his side.

"What's wrong?" she asked, her voice scratchy.

He breathed out a bitter laugh. "You're pregnant, aren't you?"

Happiness billowed inside her, then just as quickly died away. Oh, Lord, here she'd been thinking he was just searching for a way to apologize for last night before he left. This was a complication she hadn't foreseen.

She gave him a quick sidelong glance. His jaw was set like granite, and it didn't take a genius to see he wasn't happy about the situation. In fact, he was extremely disturbed. Her instincts had been right, then. With his future in place, he now felt trapped and resentful.

"H-how did you find out?" she stammered.

"I was putting away some of your things this morning and opened the wrong drawer."

Marion gripped her arms, feeling cold despite the warm sunlight pouring over them. "I'm sorry you found out."

"I bet you are." The bitterness in his voice cut her like a scythe.

"I *am.* I was hoping you'd be able to start your new life unencumbered. I didn't want you feeling guilty or trapped. I still don't." Her eyes burned with unshed tears.

Geoff paused, staring at her narrowly. "Marion, what are you talking about?"

"Nothing. Look, just go and be happy. As hurt as I am, I do want the best for you. I always have."

"And why, may I ask, are *you* hurt?"

Her head jerked around. "I'm not supposed to be hurt that my husband's fallen in love with somebody else and is planning to move three thousand miles away?"

Geoff looked thunderstruck. Emotions jostled in his eyes, but otherwise he stood absolutely still.

Remorse gripped her immediately. She sighed. "Now I've gone and done exactly what I said I didn't want to do—made you feel guilty. Forget what I just said. I'm fine, really."

But she wasn't fine, and she knew it. Even as she was tugging off her wedding band, she had to bite her lower lip to keep it from quivering.

Geoff's dark eyes widened in horror. "What are you doing?" He seemed to be inhaling the words.

"Here." Smiling bravely, she lifted his hand and folded his fingers around the ring. "I'll be fine." She didn't know where she was getting the strength to keep from breaking down. "Have a wonderful life."

She began to walk away, back to the house, but Geoff reached out and caught her wrist.

"Whoa! Hold it!" He squeezed so hard his fingers trembled.

"What?"

"What? This is hardly what I call talking, Marion."

She looked aside, unable to hold his angry stare. "You're right. Go ahead. Say what you have to."

Geoff pulled her closer, forcing her to look up at him. "Am I supposed to believe you didn't tell me we're expecting a baby because you wanted me to...to go off and be happy? Do you really think I'm that naive?"

"Well, why else would I keep news like that to myself?"

"That's what I've been wondering, too."

"Seems you know the answer," she said. "Why not let me in on it?"

He gave her arm a little shove, releasing her. "How about—you didn't tell me because you just don't want me in your life anymore. I've become unnecessary baggage. You've become so damned independent you don't even need a father for your child."

Marion opened her mouth, but nothing came out. She felt as if she'd been stabbed.

"Say something, Marion." His voice grated with derision. "Wrap me up in another one of your warm fuzzy sentiments about wanting the best for me."

Finally Marion found her voice, but all she could say before it deserted her again was, "You big jerk!" She spun around, facing the river, fighting back tears, but it was a losing battle. Suddenly grief overwhelmed her, grief for the past, grief for the future, grief for all the expectations they'd begun their marriage with that would never be realized.

"Come on, Marion. The least we can do is end this with honesty."

She swung around, hurt that he could be so cruel when she was in such obvious pain, and angry that he could so misinterpret her motives. "I didn't tell you about the baby because I'm going to lose it."

Geoff froze. "What did you say?"

"I've already had two miscarriages. This pregnancy is bound to end like the others." Feelings of failure overwhelmed her, and several seconds passed before she could continue. "I know how disappointed you were the other times, and I didn't want you to go through all that again."

"So you intended to have the miscarriage and keep that a secret, too." He swallowed, looking away. "What did you think? That I wouldn't be able to handle it? That I wouldn't hang in or stand by you?"

"No!" Marion plunged her fingers into her hair. "You'd been through enough and... and I didn't want you to resent me any more than you already did."

His eyebrows lowered. "Resent you? Why the hell would I resent you?"

"Well..." Words clogged in her throat, painful words, painful memories. "Isn't it obvious? I'm pretty useless when it comes to providing the kind of life you expected."

Geoff dropped a hand on top of his head as if it might blow off. "Oh, Marion, does all our trouble come down to our not being able to have children?"

She gulped, looking aside. "Isn't that why you lost interest in me?"

"Lost interest?"

Her lips quivered. "You know, after we gave up trying to conceive. You changed. You became, well, distant. You started working longer hours, spending more time with colleagues and very little with me."

Geoff looked at her, his mouth open, looked away, looked back and laughed incredulously. "Marion, you're the one who changed. As soon as you were free of the prospect of having children, you blossomed. You hooked up with those people in the co-op, you bought your parents' store, you became this incredibly gifted artist... I thought *you* resented *me.*"

"Why?" Her voice leapt with incredulity.

"Dozens of reasons. For marrying you before you graduated from college. For interrupting your career. For wanting a family. For the pain you suffered trying to have one. For not having the stomach to continue—"

"I didn't resent you!" she said earnestly.

"And I *never* lost interest."

"Then... what happened?"

They stared at each other a long breathless while. Finally Geoff lifted a hand to her and whispered shakily, "Oh, baby, come here."

She did. In fact, she ran, and they wrapped themselves in the shelter of each other's arms, holding on as if they might never let go.

"Maybe we both changed," Marion said after a while. "Bronwyn tried to tell me we seemed intent on running in opposite directions after we stopped going to the clinic. Do you think she was right?"

"Could be." He sighed, pulling back. "If you want to know the truth, I hated all those tests and procedures. I know that isn't a very laudable attitude. Those procedures help couples have babies all the time, and I should've had more staying power. But I hated them. I found them embarrassing and dehumanizing, and after a while, I felt like a thing, another piece of lab equipment. When we stopped going, I was relieved. I'm sorry, Marion, but I was."

Marion lifted her tentative hand and carefully laid it on his cheek. "I felt the very same."

"You did?"

"Yes. By the time we stopped, I felt like a total failure. A big zero." Marion's back straightened with an unexpected thought. "But then there was my work," she said, her voice lilting with surprise, "where I could create and produce and be in control. Where I could feel like a success again. So easily, too. That's why I cluttered my life with all that activity, Geoff. I just needed to feel better about myself."

Geoff's mouth curved downward as he brushed the back of his hand over her wet cheek. "I had no idea. Marion, I'm really sorry. I was so wrapped up in my own feelings I didn't recognize that you were going through the same kind of crisis." He pulled her to him again, tucking her head under his chin. "Basically I must've reacted the same way. Turned to my work to forget what we'd been through. Although to be honest, a lot of my attitude was reactionary—a defense against the indifference I thought you were feeling toward me."

Marion experienced a rush of light-headedness. "What a pair! What we should've done was pack a bag and take a long vacation."

"You're right. Should've sat on a beach somewhere and talked."

"Instead, we turned away—to new people, more work—"

"And in the process created a worse problem than the original," Geoff said. "We drifted, and our isolation allowed a devious person like Tiffany to come between us."

Marion frowned. "Devious?"

"You better believe it. Come here, sweetheart." He tugged her toward the hammock. "We've got a lot of talking to do about that woman."

And they did. Nearly an hour's worth. When they were done, Marion finally felt vindicated and Geoff felt relieved. Now they understood the insidious tactics Tiffany had employed to undermine Marion's confidence in herself and her trust in him.

"One question," Marion drawled, lying lazily in Geoff's arms. "If we had split and you'd gone out to California, would Tiffany have gotten anywhere with you?"

"You have to ask?"

"Well, she *is* awfully smart and pretty."

"Yes, and nice to work with, but I could never love her. Lord, Marion, the woman never stops to smell the laundry!"

"What?" Marion scrunched her nose.

"You do, you know. It's just one of the small illogical reasons I love you." Suddenly his expression crumbled and he drew her to him. "It hurt so much, Marion, being cut out of your life. It hurt so damned much." His hold tightened. "Not talking, not sharing. The isolation drove me crazy."

"Me, too. Let's never make that mistake again."

"That's a promise you can count on. Even my work suffered. All through the Seatham negotiations, my head was telling me what I was doing was ethical, but here—" his hand covered his heart "—it didn't feel right because you weren't on my side. I felt so damned incomplete."

Marion smiled softly. "I haven't admitted this to anyone yet, but I've sorta come around to appreciating your view of the Seatham development. It's tasteful, a good use of the land. My only lingering concern is the woodlands."

"And I'm working on it."

"How?" She swung her weight over him so that the hammock rocked precariously.

Laughter rumbled beneath her. "Funny how nobody ever mentioned all the Native American artifacts that've been found in those woods over the years."

"Yeah? What does that have to do with anything?"

"Well, the last thing a developer wants to hear is he's sitting on an old Indian burial ground."

Marion gaped. "There's an Indian burial ground out there?"

Geoff shrugged. "Seems likely—likely enough that Seatham's become skittish about hanging on to those woods. Don't be surprised if the Conservation Commission gets a call soon to see if it's still interested in cutting a deal." His eyes clouded momentarily. "That's the reason for all the phone calls this week between me and Tiffany. Fortunately this is our last business transaction. This time next week she'll be three thousand miles away and we'll never have to see her again."

Marion rolled off him and got out of the hammock. "Are you sure you don't want to follow her?" she asked, gazing over the river.

"Of course. You can't still doubt—"

"No, I mean the work. Tiffany told me you were tired of the small-town cases you get here in Eternity. Was she right? I mean, you're obviously such a gifted lawyer. Do you feel wasted here?"

He got out of the hammock, coming to stand beside her. "Not at all. I happen to take pride in serving my neighbors, thank you, and not all my clients are small. No, being a lawyer in Eternity fills just about every dream I ever had—professionally speaking. But the job, the town..." He shook his head. "They're nothing if I can't have you, too."

Marion's breath caught raggedly. "Are you sure? Are you quite sure? We may never have a child."

He sighed deeply. "Is it really so hard for you to believe I love you just for yourself?"

"It's... Yes, it's hard."

He framed her face with his hands, his thumbs stroking her jaw. "I swear I do, and I always have. Don't you ever doubt it. A child would only enhance what we have between us now."

"Oh, Geoff, I love you so very much." She fell against him, holding him tight. "And don't you ever doubt that I need you, too. I do, terribly."

He kissed the side of her face, her eyes, her jaw. Then his mouth found hers and didn't let go for a very long time.

"I'll tell you what I *don't* need," Marion said, nuzzling into his neck. "I don't need Center Jewelers. My jewelry designing is all the work I ever wanted, all the work I can comfortably handle, too, but I don't know how to tell my father. That store was his pride and joy. I don't know how he'll react to my selling it to a stranger."

"Then don't."

Marion tipped back her head.

"This weekend your father told me he and your mother are thinking of moving back to Eternity. They've finally decided they're bored out of their minds."

"I *told* them they were too young to retire."

"Good, because your father didn't know how to ask you if you had a place for him in the store."

"A place? He can have the entire operation back!" She whooped joyously.

Suddenly she noticed Geoff's eyes gleam with a smile that had nothing to do with her parents' return. "What?" she asked.

His grin broadened. "You're pregnant. It's just sinking in. Marion, you're pregnant."

Her stomach quavered. "Yes, for a while."

"Did Dr. Toomey tell you you were going to lose the baby?"

"Well . . . not really."

"Then where did you get the idea?"

"I just have a feeling. Given my track record... Now see! This is why I didn't want to tell you. You're already wearing a silly expectant-father grin."

"Sorry." He wiped a hand down his face. "Well, whatever happens, you've got to know I'll always be here for you. I'm going to be part of this every step of the way. If we go full term, or if we lose it. This is *our* life, Marion. Not just yours, not just mine. Ours. As Bronwyn said, we need to hang on to each other in times of crisis. Okay?"

She nodded, smiling through tears. Out of the blue she remembered something. "Geoff, my ring."

She saw his face drop. His hands patted pockets, dug into them, and finally he said, "Marion, I don't remember what I did with it. I was so stunned. Maybe I dropped it."

Marion looked at the vast expanse of lawn and wailed, "Oh, no! What did I do? That ring means the world to me."

"We'd better find it, then, hadn't we?"

Nearly fifteen minutes passed and Marion was close to hysteria when Geoff finally gave a triumphant shout. She glanced up from the area she was combing to find him holding up her wide gold band. She flopped onto her back in boneless relief.

He came over and sat beside her. She giggled, smiling up at the morning sky while the sun beamed down a benediction.

"The gods have given us too many breaks, Geoff. We're pressing our luck."

"No such thing. We were married in the Eternity chapel, remember."

She sat up, her expression sobering. "Geoff, do you believe in the legend?"

He stared at her ring, glinting between his thumb and index finger. "I'm coming around," he admitted with a small crooked smile. "But I'll tell you what I do believe in without a shadow of a doubt."

"What's that?"

His dark intense eyes captured hers. "I believe in us."

She knew the moment was special, a moment that had something to do with magic and casting new spells. But all she could reply was, "So do I."

"Then give me your hand, Mrs. Kent."

Marion lifted her left hand and he took it firmly in his. Then he slipped her wedding band onto her third finger where it belonged.

Still holding her hand, he dipped his head and kissed her mouth, a sweet loving kiss that spoke of unbounded hope and trust in the future. They were infinitely lucky. They'd nearly destroyed their marriage, yet they'd emerged like tempered steel.

"What would you like for breakfast?" she asked, getting to her feet. "We have lots of croissants and Danish left from yesterday. Or would you prefer... What?" she asked suspiciously, noticing the glint in his eyes.

He pulled her against him as they walked toward the house. "How about we forgo breakfast and find something else to do the next couple of hours?"

"Sure. How about a game of Monopoly, or were you thinking more in terms of...?" Her laughter, as he swung her off her feet, silvered the air.

And down below the yard, the river went sliding by, through Eternity and into forever.

INDULGE A LITTLE 6947 SWEEPSTAKES
NO PURCHASE NECESSARY

HERE'S HOW THE SWEEPSTAKES WORKS:
The Harlequin Reader Service shipments for January, February and March 1994 will contain, respectively, coupons for entry into three prize drawings: a trip for two to San Francisco, an Alaskan cruise for two and a trip for two to Hawaii. To be eligible for any drawing using an Entry Coupon, simply complete and mail according to directions.

There is no obligation to continue as a Reader Service subscriber to enter and be eligible for any prize drawing. You may also enter any drawing by hand printing your name and address on a 3" x 5" card and the destination of the prize you wish that entry to be considered for (i.e., San Francisco trip, Alaskan cruise or Hawaiian trip). Send your 3" x 5" entries to: Indulge a Little 6947 Sweepstakes, c/o Prize Destination you wish that entry to be considered for, P.O. Box 1315, Buffalo, NY 14269-1315, U.S.A. or Indulge a Little 6947 Sweepstakes, P.O. Box 610, Fort Erie, Ontario L2A 5X3, Canada.

To be eligible for the San Francisco trip, entries must be received by 4/30/94; for the Alaskan cruise, 5/31/94; and the Hawaiian trip, 6/30/94. No responsibility is assumed for lost, late or misdirected mail. Sweepstakes open to residents of the U.S. (except Puerto Rico) and Canada, 18 years of age or older. All applicable laws and regulations apply. Sweepstakes void wherever prohibited.

For a copy of the Official Rules, send a self-addressed, stamped envelope (WA residents need not affix return postage) to: Indulge a Little 6947 Rules, P.O. Box 4631, Blair, NE 68009, U.S.A.

INDR93

INDULGE A LITTLE 6947 SWEEPSTAKES
NO PURCHASE NECESSARY

HERE'S HOW THE SWEEPSTAKES WORKS:
The Harlequin Reader Service shipments for January, February and March 1994 will contain, respectively, coupons for entry into three prize drawings: a trip for two to San Francisco, an Alaskan cruise for two and a trip for two to Hawaii. To be eligible for any drawing using an Entry Coupon, simply complete and mail according to directions.

There is no obligation to continue as a Reader Service subscriber to enter and be eligible for any prize drawing. You may also enter any drawing by hand printing your name and address on a 3" x 5" card and the destination of the prize you wish that entry to be considered for (i.e., San Francisco trip, Alaskan cruise or Hawaiian trip). Send your 3" x 5" entries to: Indulge a Little 6947 Sweepstakes, c/o Prize Destination you wish that entry to be considered for, P.O. Box 1315, Buffalo, NY 14269-1315, U.S.A. or Indulge a Little 6947 Sweepstakes, P.O. Box 610, Fort Erie, Ontario L2A 5X3, Canada.

To be eligible for the San Francisco trip, entries must be received by 4/30/94; for the Alaskan cruise, 5/31/94; and the Hawaiian trip, 6/30/94. No responsibility is assumed for lost, late or misdirected mail. Sweepstakes open to residents of the U.S. (except Puerto Rico) and Canada, 18 years of age or older. All applicable laws and regulations apply. Sweepstakes void wherever prohibited.

For a copy of the Official Rules, send a self-addressed, stamped envelope (WA residents need not affix return postage) to: Indulge a Little 6947 Rules, P.O. Box 4631, Blair, NE 68009, U.S.A.

INDR93

INDULGE A LITTLE SWEEPSTAKES

OFFICIAL ENTRY COUPON

This entry must be received by: JUNE 30, 1994
This month's winner will be notified by: JULY 15, 1994
Trip must be taken between: AUGUST 31, 1994-AUGUST 31, 1995

YES, I want to win the 3-Island Hawaiian vacation for two. I understand that the prize includes round-trip airfare, first-class hotels and pocket money as revealed on the "wallet" scratch-off card.

Name______________________________

Address ____________________ Apt. __________

City______________________________

State/Prov._______________ Zip/Postal Code__________

Daytime phone number________________________
(Area Code)

Account #______________________________

Return entries with invoice in envelope provided. Each book in this shipment has two entry coupons—and the more coupons you enter, the better your chances of winning!

 MONTH3

INDULGE A LITTLE SWEEPSTAKES

OFFICIAL ENTRY COUPON

This entry must be received by: JUNE 30, 1994
This month's winner will be notified by: JULY 15, 1994
Trip must be taken between: AUGUST 31, 1994-AUGUST 31, 1995

YES, I want to win the 3-Island Hawaiian vacation for two. I understand that the prize includes round-trip airfare, first-class hotels and pocket money as revealed on the "wallet" scratch-off card.

Name______________________________

Address ____________________ Apt. __________

City______________________________

State/Prov._______________ Zip/Postal Code__________

Daytime phone number________________________
(Area Code)

Account #______________________________

Return entries with invoice in envelope provided. Each book in this shipment has two entry coupons—and the more coupons you enter, the better your chances of winning!

© 1993 HARLEQUIN ENTERPRISES LTD. MONTH3